Nohow On

Nohow On

Company,

Ill Seen Ill Said,

Worstward Ho

Three Novels by Samuel Beckett

With an Introduction by S. E. Gontarski

 Grove Press, New York

Ill Seen Ill Said was first published in French as *Mal vu mal dit*
by Les Editions de Minuit, Paris, France, 1981

Published simultaneously in Canada
Printed in the United States of America
FIRST EDITION

Library of Congress Cataloging-in-Publication Data

Beckett, Samuel, 1906–
    Nohow on : three novels / by Samuel Beckett ; with an introduction
by S.E. Gontarski. — 1st ed.
        p.   cm.
    Includes bibliographical references (p.   ).
    Contents: Company — Ill seen ill said — Worstward ho.
    ISBN 0-8021-3426-2
    1. Manners and customs—Fiction. I. Title.
PR6003.E282A6   1996
823'.914—dc20   95-43710

Grove Press
841 Broadway
New York, NY 10003

10 9 8 7 6 5 4 3 2

Contents

 Introduction

The Conjuring of Something out of Nothing:
Samuel Beckett's "Closed Space" Novels

... this seemed rather to belong to some story heard long before, an instant in the life of another, ill told, ill heard, and more than half forgotten. Watt

In the mid-1960s, Samuel Beckett's fiction took a dramatic turn, away from stories featuring the compulsion to (and so solace in) motion, toward stories featuring stillness or some barely perceptible movement, at times just the breathing of a body or the trembling of a hand. These "closed space" stories often entailed little more than the perception of a figure in various postures, like an exercise in human origami. The journey theme had been a mainstay of Beckett's fiction from *Murphy* and *Watt*, and it culminated in the body of French fiction:

the four French *Stories* of 1946; the three collected novels, *Molloy, Malone Dies,* and *The Unnamable*; the fictive fragments written to move beyond the impasse of *The Unnamable,* collected as *Texts for Nothing*; and the great post–*Unnamable* novel, *How It Is.* Motion offered a degree of solace to Beckett's "omnidolent" creatures: "As long as I kept walking I didn't hear [the cries] because of the footsteps," the narrator of *First Love* reminds us. But it was the fact of movement rather than any particular destination that consoled, as the narrator of *From an Abandoned Work* makes clear: "I have never in my life been on my way anywhere, but simply on my way." The shift from journeys, a movement from and return to some shelter or haven—often "home"—to the "closed space" tales was announced in the fragments and *faux départs* that eventually developed into *All Strange Away* (1963–64) and its sibling, *Imagination Dead Imagine* (1965): "Out the door and down the road in the old hat and coat like after the war, no not that again." The more *imaginative* alternative was now: "A closed space five foot square by six high, try for him there." The change necessitated a new character as well, the nameless "him" who became Beckett's second major fictional innovation. The first was "voice," that progressive disintegration of literary character that dominated the journey fictions from *Watt* through *From an Abandoned Work* and included most of Beckett's major novels—and made occasional appearances in "closed space" tales like *Company* and *Ill Seen Ill Said*, for instance. The second was "him," or on occasion "her," "one," or "it," object of narrator's creation, the narrator himself often a creation, "devised," a "him" to someone else's imaginings.

These "closed space" tales not infrequently resulted in intractable creative difficulties, literary culs-de-sac into which Beckett had written himself, and so were abandoned.[1] As often they were unabandoned, resuscitated, revived and revised as Beckett periodically returned to his "trunk manuscripts," and that stuttering creative process of experiment and impasse, breakthrough and breakdown, was folded into the narratives themselves. These are tales designed to fail, which were continued until they did fail, and then continued a bit more. As these stories were begun, abandoned, recommenced, and ended yet again, they often existed in multiple versions, most of which were, at one time or another, published, like the abandoned *faux départ* called at one point *Fancy Dying*, which developed into two published versions in the mid-1960s, *All Strange Away* and *Imagination Dead Imagine*—and similarly, the triplet of mid-seventies "Still" stories: "Still," "Sounds," and "Still 3." These stories featured a narrative consciousness straining to see and hear images that may come from within or without, and sometimes both simultaneously, resulting in what the narrator of *Ill Seen Ill Said* calls the confusion of "That old tandem": "the confusion now between real and—how say its contrary? No matter. That old tandem. Such now the confusion between them once so twain" (72).

One of the abandoned (but unpublished) tales from the 1970s is called "Long Observation of the Ray" (1976), written apparently on the way to *Ill Seen Ill Said*, of which critic Steven Connor has said, "It forms a link between two important preoccupations in Beckett's [late] work, the preoccupation with cylinders and enclosed spaces to be found in *The Lost Ones*, "Ping," *All Strange Away* and *Closed Space* [*sic.*, i.e., the *Fizzle* "Closed Place"], and the preoccupation with the dynamics of looking which runs from *Play* and *Film* through to *Ill Seen Ill Said*"[2] and, one might add, *Worstward Ho.* These "closed space" tales feature a narrator as seeing/creating eye (and so perhaps "I"), saying the seeing. The difficulties of perception and conception, memory and imagination, and the representation of both in language become the focus of much of this late fiction, as a devouring eye, "the eye of prey" as it is called at the end of *Imagination Dead Imagine*, witnesses and consumes.

The masterwork of this period of narratological experiment, the seeing in a closed space where the homophones "seen" and "scene" are coeval, is the sequence of novels written in the early 1980s and collected here under Beckett's title, *Nohow On: Company* (1980), *Mal vu mal dit* (*Ill Seen Ill Said*) (1981), and the work Beckett deemed "untranslatable," *Worstward Ho*, (1983).[3]

Although they were written in sequence and bear a close kinship to one another, Beckett himself resisted using the word *trilogy* to describe them, as he had with his first collection of novels.[4] Although "trilogy" has since become their sobriquet, Beckett consistently rejected it. When British publisher John Calder, for instance, asked him on 29 December 1957, "May we use a general title 'Trilogy' on the jacket with the three books listed underneath?" Beckett replied on 6 January, "Not 'Trilogy', I beseech you, just the three titles and nothing else." By the end of the year, Calder still lacked a comprehensive title, and he queried Beckett again, proposing to substitute the word *trinity* for *trilogy*. "I can think of no general title," Beckett replied on 19 December 1958: "TRINITY would not do. It seems to me the three separate titles should be enough."

With his American publisher, Barney Rosset of Grove Press, Beckett took the identical position, writing on 5 May 1959: "Delighted to hear you are doing the 3 in 1 soon. Simply can't think, as I told Calder, of a general title and can't bear the thought of [the] word trilogy appearing anywhere. . . . If it's possible to present the thing without either I'd be grateful. If not I'll cudgel my fused synopses [*sic*] for a word or two to cover it all."

Both American and British editions finally appeared as *Three Novels* followed by the titles of the individual works as Beckett requested, but critics have triumphed where publishers failed. The *Three Novels* are consistently referred to as "The Trilogy," a phrase occasionally italicized as if it were the actual title of the work. Although pleased with the collection, Beckett himself consistently referred to the anthology as the "so-called trilogy."

For subsequent collections Beckett was more forthcoming, offering *No's Knife* for Calder's expanded edition of what at Grove was simply *Stories and Texts for Nothing*, *Residua* for the early "closed space" tales, and for his second collection of novels—his second "3 in 1"—Beckett "cudgeled his fused [synapses]" yet again to supply a title. As Calder notes on the jacket to the British edition, "the overall title, *Nohow On*, the last words of *Worstward Ho*, have [*sic*] been given to the trilogy by the author." Calder's use of the word "trilogy" is surprising given the correspondence above, and at least one critic, the novelist and book review editor of the *Irish Times*, John Banville, has taken him to task for such cavalier usage.[5] In fact, Banville objects to the collection in general because it fails to achieve—to his eye at least—the integration (or disintegration) of the first "trilogy," in which "each successive volume in the series consumes its predecessor, swallowing and negating it, in a way entirely consistent with Beckett's stated artistic aims. No such unity is apparent in *Nohow On*" (20). Admittedly, the aporia, disintegration, and lacerating comedy (the "mirthless laugh" of *Watt*, say, played over three volumes) of the first "so-called trilogy" are missing from the second, but certainly Beckett's aims, stated or otherwise, had decidedly changed in the intervening thirty-five years, and to measure the themes and form of the earlier against those of the latter is to ignore that fact.

Trilogy or not, the three novels of *Nohow On* form a cohesion of their own, unified, as is much of the "late" fiction, by an extended exploration of the imaginative consciousness, narratives that seem to have more in common with the spatiality of painting than the chronicity of traditional storytelling, the themes of "decreation" of the earlier trilogy replaced by "re-creation," the virtual tableaux of the latter forming, dissolving, and re-forming. But such imaginative play is not just play, not, that is, frivolous or gratuitous. As critic Frank Kermode recognized, "The imagination . . . is a form-giving power; an esemplastic power, it may require . . . to be preceded by a 'decreative' act, but it is certainly a maker of orders and concords."[6] For critic Nicholas Zurbrugg, "Beckett seems to have abandoned his early images of partially resigned, partially grotesque, and partially impassioned anguish for carefully crafted images of affection, grace and harmony."[7] In Kermode's terms, the *Nohow On* "trilogy" is a fiction of order and concord.

While the title Beckett chose for his second "3 in 1" may suggest the inevitable impasse in the ineluctable aesthetic march "ill-ward" or "worstward," the final accent of the title falls on continuation, even if regressive, as the novels offer at least the possibility of respite and even occasional pleasure in the play of mind—admittedly cunning, duplicitous, inconsistent, and dissembling, but also company. The title forms finally the classically shaped Beckettian paradox, the aporia of "how" framed by "no" and its mirror image "on." As John Banville put it, "to have *said* nohow on is already to have found a way forward" (18). It is a theme that echoes Edgar in *King Lear*, "the worst is not / So long as we can say 'This is the worst'" (IV.1, 29–30). "Nohow on," then, is less a statement of impasse than a soupçon to a discourse on method, the accent of the final "on" producing "Beckett's antithetical power to becalm and console" (Zurbrugg, 45). "From where she lies she sees Venus rise," the narrator of *Ill Seen Ill Said* tells us at the opening of that narrative, and immediately thereafter offers the brief sentence that becomes the novel's refrain, "On," a word that in *Worstward Ho* is folded into the pun "so on."

The three novels of Beckett's second "3 in 1" appeared hard upon one another in a creative burst reminiscent of Beckett's "siege in the room" of 1945–1950. On 20 November 1958, Beckett wrote nostalgically about that period to Barney Rosset while lamenting the growing professional demands on his time, particularly from the theater:

When I get back from London [where he was "overseeing" the world premiere of *Krapp's Last Tape* and helping with the revival of *Endgame* at the Royal Court Theatre] if I can't get on with any new work I'll start on the translation of *Textes pour rien*. I made a balls of the new act in French I was telling you about. I'll try it again but I'm not even sure it's viable in the present setup. I feel I'm getting more and more entangled in professionalism and self-exploitation and that it would be really better to stop altogether [i.e., theater] than to go on with that. What I need is to get back into the state of mind in 1945 when it was write or perish. But I suppose no chance of that.

By the late 1970s, Beckett would hardly have perished had he stopped writing, but he seemed to return to his creative sources to produce the novels of *Nohow On* in rapid succession, three longer works that stood almost in defiance of the contemporary critical cant that saw his work lapsing (or collapsing) into inevitable and imminent silence. Some early critics had confused Beckett's pursuit of a "literature of the unword" (a phrase he used in a 1937 letter to acquaintance Axel Kaun) with the cessation of creation, an active "unwording of the world," as critic Carla Locatelli phrases it,[8] with a passive silence, a retreat into quiescence. In the "closed space" tales, however, Beckett seemed to take some consolation and even pleasure in "unwording the world," even as the enterprise was doomed to failure given the imagination's persistence even in the face of the death of imagination. Rather than rejecting language, he seems to have continued to explore its tenacious power to represent even as it was being reduced, denuded, stripped bare. The images of the "closed space" novels (and stories) disappear, vanish, or are discarded from the virtual space of consciousness only to reappear through the imagination's ineluctable visualization and the tenacity of language to represent. Even when the imagination is dead, a perverse consciousness struggles to imagine its death, which paradox seems to have launched Beckett on the enterprise of the late, "closed space" fiction. Beckett's sudden creative expansiveness then with the *Nohow On* novels confounded those critical predictions of a lapse into silence. With the turn of a new decade Beckett seems to have disentangled his complicated life as a leading man of letters and returned to his creative sources, the wellhead he celebrated in the radio play *Words and Music*, returned to the conditions of the late 1940s and the "siege in the room" that produced the first "3 in 1."

These three late novels, then, form something of a family triptych (or trilogy, or trinity, if we must) with *Company* featuring a man/son in old age, *Ill Seen Ill Said*, a ghostly woman/mother in old age, and finally *Worstward Ho*, a nearly mystical union (anticipated in *Company* and even earlier in *From an Abandoned Work*) of father and son moving motionlessly. *Company*, the first in the series, is dominated by scenes long associated with Beckett's early life and which not only appeared periodically in his work but may have assailed him psychologically as well until the very end. The story of learning to swim at the Victorian seawater baths in Dun Loaghaire called "The Forty Foot"[9] is rendered as childhood terror in *Company*: "You stand at the tip of the high board. High above the sea" (12). The scene appeared in *Watt* as well, where the image troubled a weary Watt's dreams: ". . . into an uneasy sleep, lacerated by dreams, by dives from dreadful heights into rocky waters, before a numerous public" (222). The image or memory haunted Beckett's poem of 1930 that featured this incident, "For Future Reference": "And then the bright waters / beneath the broad board / the trembling blade of the streamlined divers / and down to our waiting / to my enforced buoyancy."[10] And according to Herbert Blau, Beckett was wrestling with just this image in the nursing home shortly before his death when he asked Blau directly, "What do you think of recurring dreams? I have one, I still have it, always had it, anyway a long time. I am up on a high board, over a water full of large rocks. . . . I have to dive through a hole in the rocks."[11]

Likewise, the scene of an inquisitive child returning with his mother from Connolly's Stores and testing her patience by raising the question about the distance of the moon from Earth is another of those recurring scenes, if not recurring dreams: "A small boy you come out of Connolly's Stores holding your mother by the hand" (6). The question engenders a sharp reply in *Company*: "she shook off your little hand and made you a cutting retort you have never forgotten" (6). The mother's retort was even sharper in "The End" (1946): "A small boy, stretching out his hands and looking up at the blue sky, asked his mother how such a thing was possible. Fuck off, she said" (*Stories and Texts for Nothing*, 50); and in *Malone Dies*: "The sky is further away than you think, is it not, mama? . . . She replied, to me her son, It is precisely as far away as it appears to be" (98). But such scenes even if rooted in Beckett's childhood are no more frequent than the persistent literary allusions to Dante and Belacqua, the Florentine lutemaker stuck in Limbo: ". . . the old lutist cause of Dante's first quarter-smile and now perhaps singing praises with some section of the blessed at last" (44). And Belacqua himself may have been the model for Beckett's "closed space" figures: "huddled with his legs drawn up within the semicircle of his arms and his head on his knees" (19), like Botticelli's illustration of him for the *Divine Comedy*.

These scenes from childhood have tempted his early biographer (among others) to suggest that *Company* (and so much of Beckett's work) was coded autobiography: "You were born on an Easter Friday after long labour" (24–25), as Beckett himself was, for example. For some critics the mother-haunted *Ill Seen Ill Said* reflects the author's struggling through images of his own mother, May Beckett, whose namesake appears in the play *Footfalls* as well. And the mystical union of father and son in *Worstward Ho* may owe much to memories of Samuel Beckett's walks with his father through the

Irish countryside (an image of which Radio Telefis Éireann's documentary *Silence to Silence* makes much). But such autobiographical emphases ignore the anti-empiricism that runs through these works, the rejection of the "verifiability" of immediate knowledge since in Beckett's fictive world all is re-presentation, always already a repetition. The search for an originary model for the fictive representations ignores or subverts the very nature of these late fictions where the narrator himself is a "Devised devisor devising it all for company." The narrator is, after all, in *Company*'s most persistent pun, "lying" from the first. Even if we identify certain of the images in Beckett's fiction as having parallels in his personal life, this information tells us little about their function in the fictions. Childhood memories, like literary allusions, are "figments," "traces," "fables," or "shades," a mix of memory, experience, desire, and imagination.

Company then, like the other "closed space" tales, is neither memoir nor autobiography, but a set of devised images of one devising images. To Beckett's mind at any rate, *Company* was an interplay of voices, a fugue between "he" or "himself," called on occasion "W" (31–33), imagining himself into existence, and an external voice addressing the hearer as "you" and on occasion "M" (31–33), the former trying to provide the latter with a history and so a life. The goal of the voice is, "To have the hearer have a past and acknowledge it" (24). The tale is then a pronominal *pas de deux*. The hearer is puzzled by the voice because it is not only sourceless but false, not his, and so the "life" not "his" either, the tale not autobiographical: "Only a small part of what is said can be verified" (3), the narrator of *Company* reminds us. Stories of what may or may not be images from the narrator's past have tended to sound to him like incidents in the life of another, a situation *Company*'s unnamed narrator shares with Watt: ". . . this seemed rather to belong to some story heard long before, an instant in the life of another, ill told, ill heard, and more than half forgotten" (*Watt*, 74). What passes for memories are images often ill seen and, of necessity, ill said. In fact, both voices of *Company* are false; that is, they are fictions, figments of imagination whose function, like much of art, is aesthetic play, company for a narrator who is finally and fundamentally "as you always were. Alone" (46). The company of *Company*, then, is not the nostalgia of memory regained, the past recaptured, but the solace of "the conjuring of something out of nothing" (39).

That memories are indistinguishable from imaginings in the process of mind, both ill seen and ill said, is as much the subject of the *Nohow On* novels as any autobiographical strain. In *Ill Seen Ill Said*, the only one of the three novels written directly in French (*Company* having been written in English, translated/transformed into French, and then retranslated into English), a desiring eye, "having no need of light to see" (50), is in relentless pursuit of a ghostly old woman whose "left hand lacks its third finger" (67) and who is "drawn to a certain spot. At times. There stands a stone. It it is draws her" (52). The closed space here is a cabin in the midst of "Chalkstones." Not only are these ghostly, imagined images ill seen, but they are ill said because the right word is always the "wrong word": "And from [the cabin] as from an evil core that the what is the wrong word the evil spread" (50). There are, in fact, two eyes in this narrative: "No longer anywhere to be seen. Nor by the eye of flesh nor by the other" (56). There is as well an "imaginary stranger" (53), and a group of witnesses. And as she walks from cabin to stone she is witnessed, "On the snow her long shadow keeps her company. The others are there. All about. The twelve. Afar. Still or receding" (55). The movement of these "guardians" is such that they always "keep her in the centre" (60).

But to see this tale, and so all the "closed space" tales, as purely fictive, imaginative play with no reference beyond itself, to an external world or a narrator's memory, say, is to oversimplify as much as to see them as veiled autobiography, and the narrator cautions against such in what amounts to a summary of the narrative. It is this mingling of memory and imagination, internal and external, fiction and its opposite that causes "confusion" through which the narrative sifts:

Already all confusion. Things and imaginings. As of always. Confusion amounting to nothing. Despite precautions. If only she could be pure figment. Unalloyed. This old so dying woman. So dead. In the madhouse of the skull and nowhere else. . . . Cooped up there with the rest. Hovel and stones. The lot. And the eye. How simple all then. If only all could be pure figment. Neither be nor been nor by any shift to be. Gently gently. On. Careful. (58)

In *Worstward Ho* the images are iller seen still and so iller said as we move worstward, but we are still in "the madhouse of the skull." As Beckett outlined the themes of *Worstward Ho* in the early drafts it was clear that in addition to the "pained body" and "combined image of man and child," we have "The perceiving head or skull. 'Germ of All.'"[12] But the term "all" already contains a paradox that threatens to block the narrative. Can the skull be "germ of all," that is, even of itself: "If of all of it too"? (97). Can it then perceive itself if there is, to adapt Jacques Derrida, no outside the skull. From what perspective, from what grounding could it then be perceived? If "All" happens inside the skull, is skull inside skull as well? Such paradoxes shift the narrative focus from image to language and the latter's complicity in the act of representation. If the pivotal word, what in "A Piece of Monologue" is called "the rip word," in *Ill Seen Ill Said* is "less," in *Worstward Ho*, like *Company*, it is "gone": "Gnawing to be gone. Less no good. Worse no good. Only one good. Gone. Gone for good. Till then gnaw on. All gnaw on. To be gone" (113). But denial reinvokes, reconstitutes the image or the world, the gone always a going. That is, writing about absence reifies absence, makes of it a presence, as writing about the impossibility of writing about absence is not the creation of silences but its representation. (Beckett's silences have always been wordy.) As the image shifts in *Worstward Ho* from skull, "germ of all," to the language representing it, the narrator tries to break free of words, for which, then, he substitutes the word "blanks"—still, however, a word—and then simply a dash, "—." But the dash, too, is representation that recalls the conventions of referring to proper names in nineteenth-century Russian fiction. The closer we come to emptying the void, of man, boy, woman, skull, the closer void itself comes to being an entity imagined in language and so no different from man or boy, woman or skull. The desire to worsen language and its images generates an expansion of imaginative activity in its attempt to order experience. The drive worstward is, thus, doomed to failure, and so all that an artist can do, Beckett has been saying for some half-century, is "Try again. Fail again. Fail better" (89).

With the "closed space" novels Beckett did something new not only with his own fiction but with fiction in general—a reduction of narrative time to points of space. With the development of the "closed space" images in the mid-1960s, Beckett turned from his own earlier work, his own narrative tradition, and thereby provided himself with enough creative thrust to sustain him for the rest of his creative life. It is an aesthetics of impoverishment, of subtraction, which finally added up to some of the most carefully crafted and emotionally poignant tales of the late modernist period. "It was his genius," notes John Banville, "to produce out of such an enterprise these moving, disconsolate, and scrupulously crafted works which rank among the greatest of world literature" (20).

NOTES

1. For a fuller account of the stories abandoned and subsequently rescued, see my "From Unabandoned Works," *Samuel Beckett: The Complete Short Prose, 1929–1989* (New York: Grove Press, 1995), 1–28.

2. Steven Connor, "Between Theatre and Theory: 'Long Observation of the Ray,'" *The Ideal Core of the Onion: Reading Beckett Archives*, ed. by John Pilling and Mary Bryden (Reading, U.K.: Beckett International Foundation, 1992), 79.

3. The work has since been translated into French by Edith Fournier as *Cap au pire* (Paris: Editions de Minuit, 1991).

4. *Molloy*, 1951 (Grove Press, 1955), *Malone meurt*, 1951 (*Malone Dies*, Grove Press, 1956), and *L'Innommable*, 1953 (*The Unnamable*, Grove Press, 1958).

5. John Banville, "The Last Word," *The New York Review of Books*, 13 August 1992, 20: "Now the term 'trilogy' is not sacrosanct, but this offhand use of it is startling, to say the least" (20).

6. Frank Kermode, *The Sense of an Ending: Studies in the Theory of Fiction* (New York: Oxford University Press, 1979), 144.

7. Nicholas Zurbrugg, "Seven Types of Postmodernism: Several Types of Samuel Beckett," *The World of Samuel Beckett* (Psychiatry and the Humanities, Volume 12), ed. by Joseph H. Smith (Baltimore: Johns Hopkins University Press, 1991), 45.

8. Carla Locatelli, *Unwording the World: Samuel Beckett's Prose Work After the Nobel Prize* (Philadelphia: University of Pennsylvania Press, 1990), *passim*.

9. For additional details and pictures of the location, see Eoin O'Brien's extraordinary pictorial survey of Beckett's Ireland, *The Beckett Country* (Dublin: The Black Cat Press, 1986), 85–87.

10. *Transition* 19–20 (June 1930): 342–43. The poem is reprinted in full in Lawrence E. Harvey, *Samuel Beckett: Poet and Critic* (Princeton: Princeton University Press, 1970), 299. Harvey traces the image through the poem, commenting in the first footnote on the poem's opening quatrain: "A clear analogy to diving from a height and penetrating beneath a surface."

11. Herbert Blau, "The Less Said," *The World of Samuel Beckett*, 218.

12. For a full account of the early drafts of *Worstward Ho*, see Andrew Renton, "*Worstward Ho* and the Ends of Representation," *The Ideal Core of the Onion*, 99–135.

 Company

A voice comes to one in the dark. Imagine.

To one on his back in the dark. This he can tell by the pressure on his hind parts and by how the dark changes when he shuts his eyes and again when he opens them again. Only a small part of what is said can be verified. As for example when he hears, You are on your back in the dark. Then he must acknowledge the truth of what is said. But by far the greater part of what is said cannot be verified. As for example when he hears, You first saw the light on such and such a day. Sometimes the two are combined as for example, You first saw the light on such and such a day and now you are on your back in the dark. A device perhaps from the incontrovertibility of the one to win credence for the other. That then is the proposition. To one on his back in the dark a voice tells of a past. With occasional allusion to a present and more rarely to a future as for example, You will end as you now are. And in another dark or in the same another devising it all for company. Quick leave him.

Use of the second person marks the voice. That of the third that cankerous other. Could he speak to and of whom the voice speaks there would be a first. But he cannot. He shall not. You cannot. You shall not.

Apart from the voice and the faint sound of his breath there is no sound. None at least that he can hear. This he can tell by the faint sound of his breath.

Though now even less than ever given to wonder he cannot but sometimes wonder if it is indeed to and of him the voice is speaking. May not there be another with him in the dark to and of whom the voice is speaking? Is he not perhaps overhearing a communication not intended for him? If he is alone on his back in the dark why does the voice not say so? Why does it never say for example, You saw the light on such and such a day and now you are alone on your back in the dark? Why? Perhaps for no other reason than to kindle in his mind this faint uncertainty and embarrassment.

Your mind never active at any time is now even less than ever so. This is the type of assertion he does not question. You saw the light on such and such a day and your mind never active at any time is now even less than ever so. Yet a certain activity of mind however slight is a necessary adjunct of company. That is why the voice does not say, You are on your back in the dark and have no mental activity of any kind. The voice alone is company but not enough. Its effect on the hearer is a necessary complement. Were it only to kindle in his mind the state of faint uncertainty and embarrassment mentioned above. But company apart this effect is clearly necessary. For were he merely to hear the voice and it to have no more effect on him than speech in Bantu or in Erse then might it not as well cease? Unless its object be by mere sound to plague one in need of silence. Or of course unless as above surmised directed at another.

***

A small boy you come out of Connolly's Stores holding your mother by the hand. You turn right and advance in silence southward along the highway. After some hundred paces you head inland and broach the long steep homeward. You make ground in silence hand in hand through the warm still summer air. It is late afternoon and after some hundred paces the sun appears above the crest of the rise. Looking up at the blue sky and then at your mother's face you break the silence asking her if it is not in reality much more distant than it appears. The sky that is. The blue sky. Receiving no answer you mentally reframe your question and some hundred paces later look up at her face again and ask her if it does not appear much less distant than in reality it is. For some reason you could never fathom this question must have angered her exceedingly. For she shook off your little hand and made you a cutting retort you have never forgotten.

If the voice is not speaking to him it must be speaking to another. So with what reason remains he reasons. To another of that other. Or of him. Or of another still. To another of that other or of him or of another still. To one on his back in the dark in any case. Of one on his back in the dark whether the same or another. So with what reason remains he reasons and reasons ill. For were the voice speaking not to him but to another then it must be of that other it is speaking and not of him or of another still. Since it speaks in the second person. Were it not of him to whom it is speaking speaking but of another it would not speak in the second person but in the third. For example, He first saw the light on such and such a day and now he is on his back in the dark. It is clear therefore that if it is not to him the voice is speaking but to another it is not of him either but of that other and none other to that other. So with what reason remains he reasons ill. In order to be company he must display a certain mental activity. But it need not be of a high order. Indeed it might be argued the lower the better. Up to a point. The lower the order of mental activity the better the company. Up to a point.

You first saw the light in the room you most likely were conceived in. The big bow window looked west to the mountain. Mainly west. For being bow it looked also a little south and a little north. Necessarily. A little south to more mountain and a little north to foothill and plain. The midwife was none other than a Dr Hadden or Haddon. Straggling grey moustache and hunted look. It being a public holiday your father left the house soon after his breakfast with a flask and a package of his favourite egg sandwiches for a tramp in the mountains. There was nothing unusual in this. But on that particular morning his love of walking and wild scenery was not the only mover. But he was moved also to take himself off and out of the way by his aversion to the pains and general unpleasantness of labour and delivery. Hence the sandwiches which he relished at noon looking out to sea from the lee of a great rock on the first summit scaled. You may imagine his thoughts before and after as he strode through the gorse and heather. When he returned at nightfall he learned to his dismay from the maid at the back door that labour was still in swing. Despite its having begun before he left the house full ten hours earlier. He at once hastened to the coachhouse some twenty yards distant where he housed his De Dion Bouton. He shut the doors behind him and climbed into the driver's seat. You may imagine his thoughts as he sat there in the dark not knowing what to think. Though footsore and weary he was on the point of setting out anew across the fields in the young moonlight when the maid came running to tell him it was over at last. Over!

You are an old man plodding along a narrow country road. You have been out since break of day and now it is evening. Sole sound in the silence your footfalls. Rather sole sounds for they vary from one to the next. You listen to each one and add it in your mind to the growing sum of those that went before. You halt with bowed head on the verge of the ditch and convert into yards. On the basis now of two steps per yard. So many since dawn to add to yesterday's. To yesteryear's. To yesteryears'. Days other than today and so akin. The giant tot in miles. In leagues. How often round the earth already. Halted too at your elbow during these computations your father's shade. In his old tramping rags. Finally on side by side from nought anew.

The voice comes to him now from one quarter and now from another. Now faint from afar and now a murmur in his ear. In the course of a single sentence it may change place and tone. Thus for example clear from above his upturned face, You first saw the light at Easter and now. Then a murmur in his ear, You are on your back in the dark. Or of course vice versa. Another trait its long silences when he dare almost hope it is at an end. Thus to take the same example clear from above his upturned face, You first saw the light of day the day Christ died and now. Then long after on his nascent hope the murmur, You are on your back in the dark. Or of course vice versa.

Another trait its repetitiousness. Repeatedly with only minor variants the same bygone. As if willing him by this dint to make it his. To confess, Yes I remember. Perhaps even to have a voice. To murmur, Yes I remember. What an addition to company that would be! A voice in the first person singular. Murmuring now and then, Yes I remember.

An old beggar woman is fumbling at a big garden gate. Half blind. You know the place well. Stone deaf and not in her right mind the woman of the house is a crony of your mother. She was sure she could fly once in the air. So one day she launched herself from a first floor window. On the way home from kindergarten on your tiny cycle you see the poor old beggar woman trying to get in. You dismount and open the gate for her. She blesses you. What were her words? God reward you little master. Some such words. God save you little master.

A faint voice at loudest. It slowly ebbs till almost out of hearing. Then slowly back to faint full. At each slow ebb hope slowly dawns that it is dying. He must know it will flow again. And yet at each slow ebb hope slowly dawns that it is dying.

Slowly he entered dark and silence and lay there for so long that with what judgement remained he judged them to be final. Till one day the voice. One day! Till in the end the voice saying, You are on your back in the dark. Those its first words. Long pause for him to believe his ears and then from another quarter the same. Next the vow not to cease till hearing cease. You are on your back in the dark and not till hearing cease will this voice cease. Or another way. As in shadow he lay and only the odd sound slowly silence fell and darkness gathered. That were perhaps better company. For what odd sound? Whence the shadowy light?

You stand at the tip of the high board. High above the sea. In it your father's upturned face. Upturned to you. You look down to the loved trusted face. He calls to you to jump. He calls, Be a brave boy. The red round face. The thick moustache. The greying hair. The swell sways it under and sways it up again. The far call again, Be a brave boy. Many eyes upon you. From the water and from the bathing place.

The odd sound. What a mercy to have that to turn to. Now and then. In dark and silence to close as if to light the eyes and hear a sound. Some object moving from its place to its last place. Some soft thing softly stirring soon to stir no more. To darkness visible to close the eyes and hear if only that. Some soft thing softly stirring soon to stir no more.

By the voice a faint light is shed. Dark lightens while it sounds. Deepens when it ebbs. Lightens with flow back to faint full. Is whole again when it ceases. You are on your back in the dark. Had the eyes been open then they would have marked a change.

Whence the shadowy light? What company in the dark! To close the eyes and try to imagine that. Whence once the shadowy light. No source. As if faintly luminous all his little void. What can he have seen then above his upturned face. To close the eyes in the dark and try to imagine that.

Another trait the flat tone. No life. Same flat tone at all times. For its affirmations. For its negations. For its interrogations. For its exclamations. For its imperations. Same flat tone. You were once. You were never. Were you ever? Oh never to have been! Be again. Same flat tone.

Can he move? Does he move? Should he move? What a help that would be. When the voice fails. Some movement however small. Were it but of a hand closing. Or opening if closed to begin. What a help that would be in the dark! To close the eyes and see that hand. Palm upward filling the whole field. The lines. The fingers slowly down. Or up if down to begin. The lines of that old palm.

There is of course the eye. Filling the whole field. The hood slowly down. Or up if down to begin. The globe. All pupil. Staring up. Hooded. Bared. Hooded again. Bared again.

If he were to utter after all? However feebly. What an addition to company that would be! You are on your back in the dark and one day you will utter again. One day! In the end. In the end you will utter again. Yes I remember. That was I. That was I then.

You are alone in the garden. Your mother is in the kitchen making ready for afternoon tea with Mrs Coote. Making the wafer-thin bread and butter. From behind a bush you watch Mrs Coote arrive. A small thin sour woman. Your mother answers her saying, He is playing in the garden. You climb to near the top of a great fir.

You sit a little listening to all the sounds. Then throw yourself off. The great boughs break your fall. The needles. You lie a little with your face to the ground. Then climb the tree again. Your mother answers Mrs Coote again saying, He has been a very naughty boy.

What with what feeling remains does he feel about now as compared to then? When with what judgement remained he judged his condition final. As well inquire what he felt then about then as compared to before. When he still moved or tarried in remains of light. As then there was no then so there is none now.

In another dark or in the same another devising it all for company. This at first sight seems clear. But as the eye dwells it grows obscure. Indeed the longer the eye dwells the obscurer it grows. Till the eye closes and freed from pore the mind inquires, What does this mean? What finally does this mean that at first sight seemed clear? Till it the mind too closes as it were. As the window might close of a dark empty room. The single window giving on outer dark. Then nothing more. No. Unhappily no. Pangs of faint light and stirrings still. Unformulable gropings of the mind. Unstillable.

Nowhere in particular on the way from A to Z. Or say for verisimilitude the Ballyogan Road. That dear old back road. Somewhere on the Ballyogan Road in lieu of nowhere in particular. Where no truck any more. Somewhere on the Ballyogan Road on the way from A to Z. Head sunk totting up the tally on the verge of the ditch. Foothills to left. Croker's Acres ahead. Father's shade to right and a little to the rear. So many times already round the earth. Topcoat once green stiff with age and grime from chin to insteps. Battered once buff block hat and quarter boots still a match. No other garments if any to be seen. Out since break of day and night now falling. Reckoning ended on together from nought anew. As if bound for Stepaside. When suddenly you cut through the hedge and vanish hobbling east across the gallops.

For why or? Why in another dark or in the same? And whose voice asking this? Who asks, Whose voice asking this? And answers, His soever who devises it all. In the same dark as his creature or in another. For company. Who asks in the end, Who asks? And in the end answers as above? And adds long after to himself, Unless another still. Nowhere to be found. Nowhere to be sought. The unthinkable last of all. Unnamable. Last person. I. Quick leave him.

The light there was then. On your back in the dark the light there was then. Sunless cloudless brightness. You slip away at break of day and climb to your hiding place on the hillside. A nook in the gorse. East beyond the sea the faint shape of high mountain. Seventy miles away according to your Longman. For the third or fourth time in your life. The first time you told them and were derided. All you had seen was cloud. So now you hoard it in your heart with the rest. Back home at nightfall supperless to bed. You lie in the dark and are back in that light. Straining out from your nest in the gorse with your eyes across the water till they ache. You close them while you count a hundred. Then open and strain again. Again and again. Till in the end it is there. Palest blue against the pale sky. You lie in the dark and are back in that light. Fall asleep in that sunless cloudless light. Sleep till morning light.

Deviser of the voice and of its hearer and of himself. Deviser of himself for company. Leave it at that. He speaks of himself as of another. He says speaking of himself, He speaks of himself as of another. Himself he devises too for company. Leave it at that. Confusion too is company up to a point. Better hope deferred than none. Up to a point. Till the heart starts to sicken. Company too up to a point. Better a sick heart than none. Till it starts to break. So speaking of himself he concludes for the time being, For the time being leave it at that.

In the same dark as his creature or in another not yet imagined. Nor in what position. Whether standing or sitting or lying or in some other position in the dark. There are among the matters yet to be imagined. Matters of which as yet no inkling. The test is company. Which of the two darks is the better company. Which of all imaginable positions has the most to offer in the way of company. And similarly for the other matters yet to be imagined. Such as if such decisions irreversible. Let him for example after due imagination decide in favour of the supine position or prone and this in practice prove less companionable than anticipated. May he then or may he not replace it by another? Such as huddled with his legs drawn up within the semicircle of his arms and his head on his knees. Or in motion. Crawling on all fours. Another in another dark or in the same crawling on all fours devising it all for company. Or some other form of motion. The possible encounters. A dead rat. What an addition to company that would be! A rat long dead.

Might not the hearer be improved? Made more companionable if not downright human. Mentally perhaps there is room for enlivement. An attempt at reflexion at least. At recall. At speech even. Conation of some kind however feeble. A trace of emotion. Signs of distress. A sense of failure. Without loss of character. Delicate ground. But physically? Must he lie inert to the end? Only the eyelids stirring on and off since technically they must. To let in and shut out the dark. Might he not cross his feet? On and off. Now left on right and now a little

later the reverse. No. Quite out of keeping. He lie with
crossed feet? One glance dispels. Some movement of the
hands? A hand. A clenching and unclenching. Difficult
to justify. Or raised to brush away a fly. But there are
no flies. Then why not let there be? The temptation is
great. Let there be a fly. For him to brush away. A live
fly mistaking him for dead. Made aware of its error and
renewing it incontinent. What an addition to company
that would be! A live fly mistaking him for dead. But
no. He would not brush away a fly.

You take pity on a hedgehog out in the cold and put it
in an old hatbox with some worms. This box with the
hog inside you then place in a disused hutch wedging
the door open for the poor creature to come and go at
will. To go in search of food and having eaten to regain
the warmth and security of its box in the hutch. There
then is the hedgehog in its box in the hutch with enough
worms to tide it over. A last look to make sure all is as it
should be before taking yourself off to look for something else to pass the time heavy already on your hands
at that tender age. The glow at your good deed is slower
than usual to cool and fade. You glowed readily in those

days but seldom for long. Hardly had the glow been kindled by some good deed on your part or by some little triumph over your rivals or by a word of praise from your parents or mentors when it would begin to cool and fade leaving you in a very short time as chill and dim as before. Even in those days. But not this day. It was on an autumn afternoon you found the hedgehog and took pity on it in the way described and you were still the better for it when your bedtime came. Kneeling at your bedside you included it the hedgehog in your detailed prayer to God to bless all you loved. And tossing in your warm bed waiting for sleep to come you were still faintly glowing at the thought of what a fortunate hedgehog it was to have crossed your path as it did. A narrow clay path edged with sere box edging. As you stood there wondering how best to pass the time till bedtime it parted the edging on the one side and was making straight for the edging on the other when you entered its life. Now the next morning not only was the glow spent but a great uneasiness had taken its place. A suspicion that all was perhaps not as it should be. That rather than do as you did you had perhaps better let good alone and the hedgehog pursue its way. Days if not weeks passed before you could bring yourself to return to the hutch. You have never forgotten what you found then. You are on your back in the dark and have never forgotten what you found then. The mush. The stench.

Impending for some time the following. Need for company not continuous. Moments when his own unrelieved a relief. Intrusion of voice at such. Similarly image of hearer. Similarly his own. Regret then at having brought them about and problem how dispel them. Finally what meant by his own unrelieved? What possible relief? Leave it at that for the moment.

Let the hearer be named H. Aspirate. Haitch. You Haitch are on your back in the dark. And let him know his name. No longer any question of his overhearing. Of his not being meant. Though logically none in any case. Of words murmured in his ear to wonder if to him! So he is. So that faint uneasiness lost. That faint hope. To one with so few occasions to feel. So inapt to feel. Asking nothing better in so far as he can ask anything than to feel nothing. Is it desirable? No. Would he gain thereby in companionability? No. Then let him not be named H. Let him be again as he was. The hearer. Unnamable. You.

Imagine closer the place where he lies. Within reason. To its form and dimensions a clue is given by the voice afar. Receding afar or there with abrupt saltation or resuming there after pause. From above and from all sides and levels with equal remoteness at its most remote. At no time from below. So far. Suggesting one lying on the floor of a hemispherical chamber of generous diameter with ear dead centre. How generous? Given faintness of voice at its least faint some sixty feet should suffice or thirty from ear to any given point of encompassing surface. So much for form and dimensions. And composition? What and where clue to that if any anywhere. Reserve for the moment. Basalt is tempting. Black basalt. But reserve for the moment. So he imagines to himself as voice and hearer pall. But further imagination shows him to have imagined ill. For with what right affirm of a faint sound that it is a less faint made fainter by farness and not a true faint near at hand? Or of a faint fading to fainter that it recedes and not in situ decreases. If with none then no light from the voice on the place where our old hearer lies. In immeasurable dark. Contourless. Leave it at that for the moment. Adding only, What kind of imagination is this so reason-ridden? A kind of its own.

Another devising it all for company. In the same dark as his creature or in another. Quick imagine. The same.

Might not the voice be improved? Made more companionable. Say changing now for some time past though no tense in the dark in that dim mind. All at once over and in train and to come. But for the other say for some time past some improvement. Same flat tone as initially imagined and same repetitiousness. No improving those. But less mobility. Less variety of faintness. As if seeking optimum position. From which to discharge with greatest effect. The ideal amplitude for effortless audition. Neither offending the ear with loudness nor through converse excess constraining it to strain. How far more companionable such an organ than it initially in haste imagined. How far more likely to achieve its object. To have the hearer have a past and acknowledge it. You were

born on an Easter Friday after long labour. Yes I remember. The sun had not long sunk behind the larches. Yes
I remember. As best to erode the drop must strike un-
wavering. Upon the place beneath.

The last time you went out the snow lay on the ground.
You now on your back in the dark stand that morning
on the sill having pulled the door gently to behind you.
You lean back against the door with bowed head making ready to set out. By the time you open your eyes
your feet have disappeared and the skirts of your greatcoat come to rest on the surface of the snow. The dark
scene seems lit from below. You see yourself at that last
outset leaning against the door with closed eyes waiting for the word from you to go. To be gone. Then the
snowlit scene. You lie in the dark with closed eyes and
see yourself there as described making ready to strike out
and away across the expanse of light. You hear again the
click of the door pulled gently to and the silence before
the steps can start. Next thing you are on your way across
the white pasture afrolic with lambs in spring and strewn
with red placentae. You take the course you always take
which is a beeline for the gap or ragged point in the

quickset that forms the western fringe. Thither from your entering the pasture you need normally from eighteen hundred to two thousand paces depending on your humour and the state of the ground. But on this last morning many more will be required. Many many more. The beeline is so familiar to your feet that if necessary they could keep to it and you sightless with error on arrival of not more than a few feet north or south. And indeed without any such necessity unless from within this is what they normally do and not only here. For you advance if not with closed eyes though this as often as not at least with them fixed on the momentary ground before your feet. That is all of nature you have seen. Since finally you bowed your head. The fleeting ground before your feet. From time to time. You do not count your steps any more. For the simple reason they number each day the same. Average day in day out the same. The way being always the same. You keep count of the days and every tenth day multiply. And add. Your father's shade is not with you any more. It fell out long ago. You do not hear your footfalls any more. Unhearing unseeing you go your way. Day after day. The same way. As if there were no other any more. For you there is no other any more. You used never to halt except to make your reckoning. So as to plod on from nought anew. This need removed as we have seen there is none in theory to halt any more. Save perhaps a moment at the outermost point. To gather yourself together for the return. And yet you do. As never before. Not for tiredness. You are no more tired now than you always were. Not because of age. You are no older now than you always were. And yet you halt as never before. So that the same hundred yards you used to cover in a matter of three to four minutes may now take you anything from fifteen to twenty. The foot falls unbidden in midstep or next for lift cleaves to the ground bringing the body to a stand. Then a speechlessness whereof the gist, Can they go on? Or better, Shall they go on? The barest gist. Stilled when finally as always hitherto they do. You lie in the dark with closed eyes and see the scene. As you could not at the time. The dark cope of sky. The dazzling land. You at a standstill in the midst. The quarter boots sunk to the tops. The skirts of the greatcoat resting on the snow. In the old bowed head in the old block hat speechless misgiving. Halfway across the pasture on your beeline to the gap. The unerring feet fast. You look behind you as you could not then and see their trail. A great swerve. Withershins. Almost as if all at once the heart too heavy. In the end too heavy.

Bloom of adulthood. Imagine a whiff of that. On your back in the dark you remember. Ah you you remember. Cloudless May day. She joins you in the little summerhouse. A rustic hexahedron. Entirely of logs. Both larch and fir. Six feet across. Eight from floor to vertex. Area twenty-four square feet to furthest decimal. Two small multicoloured lights vis-à-vis. Small stained diamond panes. Under each a ledge. There on summer Sundays after his midday meal your father loved to retreat with *Punch* and a cushion. The waist of his trousers unbuttoned he sat on the one ledge turning the pages. You on the other with your feet dangling. When he chuckled you tried to chuckle too. When his chuckle died yours too. That you should try to imitate his chuckle pleased and tickled him greatly and sometimes he would chuckle for no other reason than to hear you try to chuckle too. Sometimes you turn your head and look out through a rose-red pane. You press your little nose against the pane and all without is rosy. The years have

flown and there at the same place as then you sit in the
bloom of adulthood bathed in rainbow light gazing
before you. She is late. You close your eyes and try to
calculate the volume. Simple sums you find a help in
times of trouble. A haven. You arrive in the end at seven
cubic yards approximately. Even still in the timeless dark
you find figures a comfort. You assume a certain heart
rate and reckon how many thumps a day. A week. A
month. A year. And assuming a certain lifetime a lifetime. Till the last thump. But for the moment with
hardly more than seventy American billion behind you
you sit in the little summerhouse working out the volume. Seven cubic yards approximately. This strikes you
for some reason as improbable and you set about your
sun anew. But you have not made much headway when
her light step is heard. Light for a woman of her size.
You open with quickening pulse your eyes and a moment later that seems an eternity her face appears at the
window. Mainly blue in this position the natural pallor
you so admire as indeed from it no doubt wholly blue
your own. For natural pallor is a property you have in
common. The violet lips do not return your smile. Now
this window being flush with your eyes from where you
sit and the floor as near as no matter with the outer

ground you cannot but wonder if she has not sunk to her knees. Knowing from experience that the height or length you have in common is the sum of equal segments. For when bolt upright or lying at full stretch you cleave face to face then your knees meet and your pubes and the hairs of your heads mingle. Does it follow from this that the loss of height for the body that sits is the same as for it that kneels? At this point assuming height of seat adjustable as in the case of certain piano stools you close your eyes the better with mental measure to measure and compare the first and second segments namely from sole to knee-pad and thence to pelvic girdle. How given you were both moving and at rest to the closed eye in your waking hours! By day and by night. To that perfect dark. That shadowless light. Simply to be gone. Or for affair as now. A single leg appears. Seen from above. You separate the segments and lay them side by side. It is as you half surmised. The upper is the longer and the sitter's loss the greater when seat at knee level. You leave the pieces lying there and open your eyes to find her sitting before you. All dead still. The ruby lips do not return your smile. Your gaze descends to the breasts. You do not remember them so big. To the abdomen. Same impression. Dissolve to your father's straining against the unbuttoned waistband. Can it be she is with child without your having asked for as much as her hand? You go back into your mind. She too did you but know it has closed her eyes. So you sit face to face in the little summerhouse. With eyes closed and your hands on your pubes. In that rainbow light. That dead still.

Wearied by such stretch of imagining he ceases and all ceases. Till feeling the need for company again he tells himself to call the hearer M at least. For readier reference. Himself some other character. W. Devising it all himself included for company. In the same dark as M when last heard of. In what posture and whether fixed or mobile left open. He says further to himself referring to himself, When last he referred to himself it was to say he was in the same dark as his creature. Not in another as once seemed possible. The same. As more companionable. And that his posture there remained to be devised. And to be decided whether fast or mobile. Which of all imaginable postures least liable to pall? Which of motion or of rest the more entertaining in the long run? And in the same breath too soon to say and why after all not say without further ado what can later be unsaid and what if it could not? What then? Could he now if he chose move out of the dark he chose when last heard of and away from his creature into another? Should he now decide to lie and come later to regret it could he then rise to his feet for example and lean against a wall or pace to and fro? Could M be reimagined in an easy chair? With hands free to go to his assistance? There in the same dark as his creature he leaves himself to these perplexities while wondering as every now and then he wonders in the back of his mind if the woes of the world are all they used to be. In his day.

M so far as follows. On his back in a dark place form and dimensions yet to be devised. Hearing on and off a voice of which uncertain whether addressed to him or to another sharing his situation. There being nothing to show when it describes correctly his situation that the description is not for the benefit of another in the same situation. Vague distress at the vague thought of his perhaps overhearing a confidence when he hears for example, You are on your back in the dark. Doubts gradually dashed as voice from questing far and wide closes in upon him. When it ceases no other sound than his breath. When it ceases long enough vague hope it may have said its last. Mental activity of a low order. Rare flickers of reasoning of no avail. Hope and despair and suchlike barely felt. How current situation arrived at unclear. No that then to compare to this now. Only eyelids move. When for relief from outer and inner dark they close and open respectively. Other small local movements eventually within moderation not to be despaired of. But no improvement by means of such achieved so far. Or on a higher plane by such addition to company as a movement of sustained sorrow or desire or remorse or curiosity or anger and so on. Or by some successful act of intellection as were he to think to himself referring to himself, Since he cannot think he will give up trying. Is there anything to add to this esquisse? His unnamability. Even M must go. So W reminds himself of his creature as so far created. W? But W too is creature. Figment.

Yet another then. Of whom nothing. Devising figments to temper his nothingness. Quick leave him. Pause and again in panic to himself, Quick leave him.

Devised deviser devising it all for company. In the same figment dark as his figments. In what posture and if or not as hearer in his for good not yet devised. Is not one immovable enough? Why duplicate this particular solace? Then let him move. Within reason. On all fours. A moderate crawl torso well clear of the ground eyes front alert. If this no better than nothing cancel. If possible. And in the void regained another motion. Or none. Leaving only the most helpful posture to be devised. But to be going on with let him crawl. Crawl and fall. Crawl again and fall again. In the same figment dark as his other figments.

From ranging far and wide as if in quest the voice comes to rest and constant faintness. To rest where? Imagine warily.

Above the upturned face. Falling tangent to the crown. So that in the faint light it sheds were there a mouth to be seen he would not see it. Roll as he might his eyes. Height from the ground?

Arm's length. Force? Low. A mother's stooping over cradle from behind. She moves aside to let the father

look. In his turn he murmurs to the newborn. Flat tone
unchanged. No trace of love.

You are on your back at the foot of an aspen. In its trembling shade. She at right angles propped on her elbows
head between her hands. Your eyes opened and closed
have looked in hers looking in yours. In your dark you
look in them again. Still. You feel on your face the fringe
of her long black hair stirring in the still air. Within the
tent of hair your faces are hidden from view. She murmurs, Listen to the leaves. Eyes in each other's eyes you
listen to the leaves. In their trembling shade.

Crawling and falling then. Crawling again and falling
again. If this finally no improvement on nothing he can
always fall for good. Or have never risen to his knees.
Contrive how such crawl unlike the voice may serve to
chart the area. However roughly. First what is the unit
of crawl? Corresponding to the footstep of erect loco-
motion. He rises to all fours and makes ready to set out.
Hands and knees angles of an oblong two foot long
width irrelevant. Finally say left knee moves forward six

inches thus half halving distance between it and homologous hand. Which then in due course in its turn moves forward by as much. Oblong now rhomboid. But for no longer than it takes right knee and hand to follow suit. Oblong restored. So on till he drops. Of all modes of crawl this the repent amble is possibly the least common. And so possibly of all the most diverting.

So as he crawls the mute count. Grain by grain in the mind. One two three four one. Knee hand knee hand two. One foot. Till say after five he falls. Then sooner or later on from nought anew. One two three four one. Knee hand knee hand two. Six. So on. In what he wills a beeline. Till having encountered no obstacle discouraged he heads back the way he came. From nought anew. Or in some quite different direction. In what he hopes a beeline. Till again with no dead end for his pains he renounces and embarks on yet another course. From nought anew. Well aware or little doubting how darkness may deflect. Withershins on account of the heart. Or conversely to shortest path convert deliberate veer. Be that as it may and crawl as he will no bourne as yet. As yet imaginable. Hand knee hand knee as he will. Bourneless dark.

***

Would it be reasonable to imagine the hearer as mentally quite inert? Except when he hears. That is when the voice sounds. For what if not it and his breath is there for him to hear? Aha! The crawl. Does he hear the crawl? The fall? What an addition to company were he but to hear the crawl. The fall. The rising to all fours again. The crawl resumed. And wonder to himself what in the world such sounds might signify. Reserve for a duller moment. What if not sound could set his mind in motion? Sight? The temptation is strong to decree there is nothing to see. But too late for the moment. For he sees a change of dark when he opens or shuts his eyes. And he may see the faint light the voice imagined to shed. Rashly imagined. Light infinitely faint it is true since now no more than a mere murmur. Here suddenly seen how his eyes close as soon as the voice sounds. Should they happen to be open at the time. So light as let be faintest light no longer perceived than the time it takes the lid to fall. Taste? The taste in his mouth? Long since dulled. Touch? The thrust of the ground against his bones. All the way from calcaneum to bump of philoprogenitiveness. Might not a notion to stir ruffle his apathy? To turn on his side. On his face. For a change. Let that much of want be conceded. With attendant relief that the days are no more when he could writhe in vain. Smell? His own? Long since dulled. And a barrier to others if any. Such as might have once emitted a rat long dead. Or some other carrion. Yet to be imagined. Unless the crawler smell. Aha! The crawling creator. Might the crawling creator be reasonably imagined to smell? Even fouler than his creature. Stirring now and then to wonder that mind so lost to wonder. To wonder what in the world can be making that alien smell. Whence in the world those wafts of villainous smell. How much more companionable could his creator but smell. Could he but smell his creator. Some sixth sense? Inexplicable premonition of impending ill? Yes or no? No. Pure reason? Beyond experience. God is love. Yes or no? No.

Can the crawling creator crawling in the same create dark as his creature create while crawling? One of the questions he put to himself as between two crawls he lay. And if the obvious answer were not far to seek the most helpful was another matter. And many crawls were necessary and the like number of prostrations before he could finally make up his imagination on this score. Adding to himself without conviction in the same breath as always that no answer of his was sacred. Come what might the answer he hazarded in the end was no he could not. Crawling in the dark in the way described was too serious a matter and too all-engrossing to permit of any other business were it only the conjuring of something out of nothing. For he had not only as perhaps too hastily imagined to cover the ground in this special way but rectigrade into the bargain to the best of his ability. And furthermore to count as he went adding half foot to half foot and retain in his memory the ever-changing sum of those gone before. And finally to maintain eyes and ears at a high level of alertness for any clue however small to the nature of the place to which imagination perhaps unadvisedly had consigned him. So while in the same breath deploring a fancy so reason-ridden and observing how revocable its flights he could not but answer finally no he could not. Could not conceivably create while crawling in the same create dark as his creature.

A strand. Evening. Light dying. Soon none left to die. No. No such thing then as no light. Died on to dawn and never died. You stand with your back to the wash.

No sound but its. Ever fainter as it slowly ebbs. Till it slowly flows again. You lean on a long staff. Your hands rest on the knob and on them your head. Were your eyes to open they would first see far below in the last rays the skirt of your greatcoat and the uppers of your boots emerging from the sand. Then and it alone till it vanishes the shadow of the staff on the sand. Vanishes from your sight. Moonless starless night. Were your eyes to open dark would lighten.

Crawls and falls. Lies. Lies in the dark with closed eyes resting from his crawl. Recovering. Physically and from his disappointment at having crawled again in vain. Perhaps saying to himself, Why crawl at all? Why not just lie in the dark with closed eyes and give up? Give up all. Have done with all. With bootless crawl and figments comfortless. But if on occasion so disheartened it is seldom for long. For little by little as he lies the craving for company revives. In which to escape from his own. The need to hear that voice again. If only saying again, You are on your back in the dark. Or if only, You first saw the light and cried at the close of the day when in darkness Christ at the ninth hour cried and died. The need eyes closed the better to hear to see that glimmer shed. Or with addition of some human weakness to improve the hearer. For example an itch beyond reach of the hand or better still within while the hand immovable. An unscratchable itch. What an addition to company that would be! Or last if not least resort to ask himself what precisely he means when he speaks of himself loosely as lying. Which in other words of all the innumerable ways of lying is likely to prove in the long run the most endearing. If having crawled in the way described he falls it would normally be on his face. Indeed given the degree of his fatigue and discouragement at this point it is hard to see how he could do otherwise. But once fallen and lying on his face there is no reason why he should not turn over on one or other of his sides or on his only back and so lie should any of these three postures offer better company than any of the other three. The supine though most tempting he must finally disallow as being already supplied by the hearer. With regard to the sidelong one glance is enough to dispel them both. Leaving him with no other choice than the prone. But how prone? Prone how? How disposed the legs? The arms? The head? Prone in the dark he strains to see how best he may lie prone. How most companionably.

See hearer clearer. Which of all the ways of lying supine the least likely in the long run to pall? After long straining eyes closed prone in the dark the following. But first naked or covered? If only with a sheet. Naked. Ghostly in the voice's glimmer that bonewhite flesh for company. Head resting mainly on occipital bump aforesaid. Legs joined at attention. Feet splayed ninety degrees. Hands invisibly manacled crossed on pubis. Other details as need felt. Leave him at that for the moment.

Numb with the woes of your kind you raise none the less your head from off your hands and open your eyes. You turn on without moving from your place the light above you. Your eyes light on the watch lying beneath it. But instead of reading the hour of night they follow round and round the second hand now followed and now preceded by its shadow. Hours later it seems to you as follows. At 60 seconds and 30 seconds shadow hidden by hand. From 60 to 30 shadow precedes hand at a distance increasing from zero at 60 to maximum at 15 and thence decreasing to new zero at 30. From 30 to 60 shadow follows hand at a distance increasing from zero at 30 to maximum at 45 and thence decreasing to

new zero at 60. Slant light now to dial by moving either
to either side and hand hides shadow at two quite different points as for example 50 and 20. Indeed at any
two quite different points whatever depending on degree of slant. But however great or small the slant and
more or less remote from initial 60 and 30 the new
points of zero shadow the space between the two remains one of 30 seconds. The shadow emerges from
under hand at any point whatever of its circuit to follow or precede it for the space of 30 seconds. Then
disappears infinitely briefly before emerging again to
precede or follow it for the space of 30 seconds again.
And so on and on. This would seem to be the one constant. For the very distance itself between hand and
shadow varies as the degree of slant. But however great
or small this distance it invariably waxes and wanes from
nothing to a maximum 15 seconds later and to nothing
again 15 seconds later again respectively. And so on and
on. This would seem to be a second constant. More
might have been observed on the subject of this second
hand and its shadow in their seemingly endless parallel
rotation round and round the dial and other variables
and constants brought to light and errors if any corrected
in what had seemed so far. But unable to continue you

bow your head back to where it was and with closed eyes return to the woes of your kind. Dawn finds you still in this position. The low sun shines on you through the eastern window and flings all along the floor your shadow and that of the lamp left lit above you. And those of other objects also.

What visions in the dark of light! Who exclaims thus? Who asks who exclaims, What visions in the shadeless dark of light and shade! Yet another still? Devising it all for company. What a further addition to company that would be! Yet another still devising it all for company. Quick leave him.

Somehow at any price to make an end when you could go out no more you sat huddled in the dark. Having covered in your day some twenty-five thousand leagues or roughly thrice the girdle. And never once overstepped a radius of one from home. Home! So sat waiting to be purged the old lutist cause of Dante's first quarter-smile and now perhaps singing praises with some section of the blest at last. To whom here in any case farewell. The place is windowless. When as you sometimes do to void the fluid you open your eyes dark lessens. Thus you now on your back in the dark once sat huddled there your body having shown you it could go out no more. Out no more to walk the little winding back roads and interjacent pastures now alive with flocks and now deserted. With at your elbow for long years your father's shade in his old tramping rags and then for long years alone. Adding step after step to the ever mounting sum of those already accomplished. Halting now and then with bowed head to fix the score. Then on from nought anew. Huddled thus you find yourself imagining you are not alone while knowing full well that nothing has occurred to make this possible. The process continues none the less lapped as it were in its meaninglessness. You do not murmur in so many words, I know this doomed to fail and yet persist. No. For the first personal singular and a fortiori plural pronoun had never any place in your vocabulary. But without a word you view yourself to this effect as you would a stranger suffering say from Hodgkin's disease or if you prefer Percival Pott's surprised at prayer. From time to time with unexpected grace you lie. Simultaneously the various parts set out. The arms unclasp the knees. The head lifts. The legs start to straighten. The trunk tilts backward. And together these and countless others continue on their respective ways till they can go no further and together come to rest. Supine now you resume your fable where the act of lying cut it short. And persist till the converse operation cuts it short again. So in the dark now huddled and now supine you toil in vain. And just as from the former position to the latter the shift grows easier in time and more alacrious so from the latter to the former the reverse is true. Till from the occasional relief it was supineness becomes habitual and finally the rule. You now on your back in the dark shall not rise to your arse again to clasp your legs in your arms and bow down your head till it can bow down no further. But with face upturned for good labour in vain at your fable. Till finally you hear how words are coming to an end. With every inane word a little nearer to the last. And how the fable too. The fable of one with you in the dark. The fable of one fabling of one with you in the dark. And how better in the end labour lost and silence. And you as you always were.

Alone.

Ill Seen Ill Said

From where she lies she sees Venus rise. On. From where she lies when the skies are clear she sees Venus rise followed by the sun. Then she rails at the source of all life. On. At evening when the skies are clear she savours its star's revenge. At the other window. Rigid upright on her old chair she watches for the radiant one. Her old deal spindlebacked kitchen chair. It emerges from out the last rays and sinking ever brighter is engulfed in its turn. On. She sits on erect and rigid in the deepening gloom. Such helplessness to move she cannot help. Heading on foot for a particular point often she freezes on the way. Unable till long after to move on not knowing whither or for what purpose. Down on her knees especially she finds it hard not to remain so forever. Hand resting on hand on some convenient support. Such as the foot of her bed. And on them her head. There then she sits as though turned to stone face to the night. Save for the white of her hair and faintly bluish white of face and hands all is black. For an eye having no need of light to see. All this in the present as had she the misfortune to be still of this world.

The cabin. Its situation. Careful. On. At the inexistent centre of a formless place. Rather more circular than otherwise finally. Flat to be sure. To cross it in a straight line takes her from five to ten minutes. Depending on her speed and radius taken. Here she who loves to—here she who now can only stray never strays. Stones increasingly abound. Ever scanter even the rankest weed. Meagre pastures hem it round on which it slowly gains. With none to gainsay. To have gainsaid. As if doomed to spread. How come a cabin in such a place? How came? Careful. Before replying that in the far past at the time of its building there was clover growing to its very walls. Implying furthermore that it the culprit. And from it as from an evil core that the what is the wrong word the evil spread. And none to urge—none to have urged its demolition. As if doomed to endure. Question answered. Chalkstones of striking effect in the light of the

moon. Let it be in opposition when the skies are clear.
Quick then still under the spell of Venus quick to the
other window to see the other marvel rise. How whiter
and whiter as it climbs it whitens more and more the
stones. Rigid with face and hands against the pane she
stands and marvels long.

The two zones form a roughly circular whole. As though
outlined by a trembling hand. Diameter. Careful. Say one
furlong. On an average. Beyond the unknown. Mercifully.
The feeling at times of being below sea level. Especially
at night when the skies are clear. Invisible nearby sea.
Inaudible. The entire surface under grass. Once clear of
the zone of stones. Save where it has receded from the
chalky soil. Innumerable white scabs all shapes and sizes.
Of striking effect in the light of the moon. In the way of
animals ovines only. After long hesitation. They are white
and make do with little. Whence suddenly come no knowing nor whither as suddenly gone. Unshepherded they
stray as they list. Flowers? Careful. Alone the odd crocus
still at lambing time. And man? Shut of at last? Alas no.
For will she not be surprised one day to find him gone?
Surprised no she is beyond surprise. How many? A fig-

ure come what may. Twelve. Wherewith to furnish the horizon's narrow round. She raises her eyes and sees one. Turns away and sees another. So on. Always afar. Still or receding. She never once saw one come toward her. Or she forgets. She forgets. Are they always the same? Do they see her? Enough.

A moor would have better met the case. Were there a case better to meet. There had to be lambs. Rightly or wrongly. A moor would have allowed of them. Lambs for their whiteness. And for other reasons as yet obscure. Another reason. And so that there may be none. At lambing time. That from one moment to the next she may raise her eyes to find them gone. A moor would have allowed of them. In any case too late. And what lambs. No trace of frolic. White splotches in the grass. Aloof from the unheeding ewes. Still. Then a moment straying. Then still again. To think there is still life in this age. Gently gently.

She is drawn to a certain spot. At times. There stands a stone. It it is draws her. Rounded rectangular block three times as high as wide. Four. Her stature now. Her lowly stature. When it draws she must to it. She cannot see it from her door. Blindfold she could find her way. With herself she has no more converse. Never had much. Now none. As had she the misfortune to be still of this world. But when the stone draws then to her feet the prayer, Take her. Especially at night when the skies are clear. With moon or without. They take her and halt her before it. There she too as if of stone. But black. Sometimes in the light of the moon. Mostly of the stars alone. Does she envy it?

To the imaginary stranger the dwelling appears deserted. Under constant watch it betrays no sign of life. The eye glued to one or the other window has nothing but black drapes for its pains. Motionless against the door he listens long. No sound. Knocks. No answer. Watches all night in vain for the least glimmer. Returns at last to his own and avows, No one. She shows herself only to her own. But she has no own. Yes yes she has one. And who has her.

There was a time when she did not appear in the zone of stones. A long time. Was not therefore to be seen going out or coming in. When she appeared only in the pastures. Was not therefore to be seen leaving them. Save as though by enchantment. But little by little she began to appear. In the zone of stones. First darkly. Then more and more plain. Till in detail she could be seen crossing the threshold both ways and closing the door behind her. Then a time when within her walls she did not appear. A long time. But little by little she began to appear. Within her walls. Darkly. Time truth to tell still current. Though she within them no more. This long time.

Yes within her walls so far at the window only. At one or the other window. Rapt before the sky. And only half seen so far a pallet and a ghostly chair. Ill half seen. And how in her faint comings and goings she suddenly stops dead. And how hard set to rise up from off her knees. But there too little by little she begins to appear more plain. Within her walls. As well as other objects. Such as under her pillow—such as deep in some recess this still shadowy album. Perhaps in time be by her when she takes it on her knees. See the old fingers fumble through the pages. And what scenes they can possibly be that draw the head down lower still and hold it in thrall. In the meantime who knows no more than withered flowers. No more!

***

But quick seize her where she is best to be seized. In the pastures far from shelter. She crosses the zone of stones and is there. Clearer and clearer as she goes. Quick seeing she goes out less and less. And so to say only in winter. Winter in her winter haunts she wanders. Far from shelter. Head bowed she makes her slow wavering way across the snow. It is evening. Yet again. On the snow her long shadow keeps her company. The others are there. All about. The twelve. Afar. Still or receding. She raises her eyes and sees one. Turns away and sees another. Again she stops dead. Now the moment or never. But something forbids. Just time to begin to glimpse a fringe of black veil. The face must wait. Just time before the eye cast down. Where nothing to be seen in the grazing rays but snow. And how all about little by little her footprints are effaced.

What is it defends her? Even from her own. Averts the intent gaze. Incriminates the dearly won. Forbids divining her. What but life ending. Hers. The other's. But so otherwise. She needs nothing. Nothing utterable.

Whereas the other. How need in the end? But how? How need in the end?

Times when she is gone. Long lapses of time. At crocus time it would be making for the distant tomb. To have that on the imagination! On top of the rest. Bearing by the stem or round her arm the cross or wreath. But she can be gone at any time. From one moment of the year to the next suddenly no longer there. No longer anywhere to be seen. Nor by the eye of flesh nor by the other. Then as suddenly there again. Long after. So on. Any other would renounce. Avow, No one. No one more. Any other than this other. In wait for her to reappear. In order to resume. Resume the—what is the word? What the wrong word?

Riveted to some detail of the desert the eye fills with tears. Imagination at wit's end spreads its sad wings. Gone she hears one night the sea as if afar. Plucks up her long skirt to make better haste and discovers her boots and stockings to the calf. Tears. Last example the flagstone before her door that by dint by dint her little weight has grooved. Tears.

***

Before left for the stockings the boots have time to be
ill buttoned. Weeping over as weeping will see now the
buttonhook larger than life. Of tarnished silver pisciform
it hangs by its hook from a nail. It trembles faintly without cease. As if here without cease the earth faintly
quaked. The oval handle is wrought to a semblance of
scales. The shank a little bent leads up to the hook the
eye so far still dry. A lifetime of hooking has lessened its
curvature. To the point at certain moments of its seem-
ing unfit for service. Child's play with a pliers to restore
it. Was there once a time she did? Careful. Once once
in a way. Till she could no more. No more bring the
jaws together. Oh not for weakness. Since when it hangs
useless from the nail. Trembling imperceptibly without
cease. Silver shimmers some evenings when the skies are
clear. Close-up then. In which in defiance of reason the
nail prevails. Long this image till suddenly it blurs.

She is there. Again. Let the eye from its vigil be distracted
a moment. At break or close of day. Distracted by the
sky. By something in the sky. So that when it resumes
the curtain may be no longer closed. Opened by her to

let her see the sky. But even without that she is there. Without the curtain's being opened. Suddenly open. A flash. The suddenness of all! She still without stopping. On her way without starting. Gone without going. Back without returning. Suddenly it is evening. Or dawn. The eye rivets the bare window. Nothing in the sky will distract it from it more. While she from within looks her fill. Pfft occulted. Nothing having stirred.

Already all confusion. Things and imaginings. As of always. Confusion amounting to nothing. Despite precautions. If only she could be pure figment. Unalloyed. This old so dying woman. So dead. In the madhouse of the skull and nowhere else. Where no more precautions to be taken. No precautions possible. Cooped up there with the rest. Hovel and stones. The lot. And the eye. How simple all then. If only all could be pure figment. Neither be nor been nor by any shift to be. Gently gently. On. Careful.

Here to the rescue two lights. Two small skylights. Set in the high-pitched roof on either side. Each shedding dim light. No ceiling therefore. Necessarily. Otherwise with the curtains closed she would be in the dark. Day and night in the dark. And what of it? She is done with raising her eyes. Nearly done. But when she lies with them open she can just make out the rafters. In the dim light the skylights shed. An even dimmer light. As the panes slowly dimmen. All in black she comes and goes. The hem of her long black skirt brushes the floor. But most often she is still. Standing or sitting. Lying or on her knees. In the dim light the skylights shed. Otherwise with the curtains closed for preference she would be in the dark. In the dark day and night.

Next to emerge from the shadows an inner wall. Only slowly to dissolve in favour of a single space. East the bed. West the chair. A place divided by her use of it alone. How more desirable in every way an interior of a piece. The eye breathes again but not for long. For slowly it emerges again. Rises from the floor and slowly up to lose itself in the gloom. The semigloom. It is evening. The button-hook glimmers in the last rays. The pallet scarce to be seen.

***

Weary of the inanimate the eye in her absence falls back on the twelve. Out of her sight as she of theirs. Alone turn where she may she keeps her eyes fixed on the ground. On the way at her feet where it has come to a stop. Winter evening. Not to be precise. All so bygone. To the twelve then for want of better the widowed eye. No matter which. In the distance stiff he stands facing front and the setting sun. Dark greatcoat reaching to the ground. Antiquated block hat. Finally the face caught full in the last rays. Quick enlarge and devour before night falls.

Having no need of light to see the eye makes haste. Before night falls. So it is. So itself belies. Then glutted—then torpid under its lid makes way for unreason. What if not her do they ring around? Careful. She who looks up no more looks up and sees them. Some among them. Still or receding. Receding. Those too closely seen who move to preserve their distance. While at the same time others advance. Those in the wake of her wandering. She never once saw one come toward her. Or she forgets. She forgets. Now some do. Toward but never nearer. Thus they keep her in the centre. More or less.

What then if not her do they ring around? In their ring whence she disappears unhindered. Whence they let her disappear. Instead of disappearing in her company. So the unreasoning goes. While the eye digests its pittance. In its private dark. In the general dark.

As hope expires of her ever reappearing she reappears. At first sight little changed. It is evening. It will always be evening. When not night. She emerges at the fringe of the pastures and sets forward across them. Slowly with fluttering step as if wanting mass. Suddenly still and as suddenly on her way again. At this rate it will be black night before she reaches home. Home! But time slows all this while. Suits its speed to hers. Whence from beginning to end of her course no loss or but little of twilight. A matter at most of a candle or two. Bearing south as best she can she casts toward the moon to come her long black shadow. They come at last to the door holding a great key. At the same instant night. When not evening night. Head bowed she stands exposed facing east. All dead still. All save hanging from a finger the old key polished by use. Trembling it faintly shimmers in the light of the moon.

***

Wooed from below the face consents at last. In the dim light reflected by the flag. Calm slab worn and polished by agelong comings and goings. Livid pallor. Not a wrinkle. How serene it seems this ancient mask. Worthy those worn by certain newly dead. True the light leaves to be desired. The lids occult the longed-for eyes. Time will tell them washen blue. Where tears perhaps not for nothing. Unimaginable tears of old. Lashes jet black remains of the brunette she was. Perhaps once was. When yet a lass. Yet brunette. Skipping the nose at the call of the lips these no sooner broached are withdrawn. The slab having darkened with the darkening sky. Black night henceforward. And at dawn an empty place. With no means of knowing whether she has gone in or under cover of darkness her ways again.

White stones more plentiful every year. As well say every instant. In a fair way if they persist to bury all. First zone rather more extensive than at first sight ill seen and every year rather more. Of striking effect in the light of the moon these millions of little sepulchres. But in her absence but cold comfort. From it then in the end to the second miscalled pastures. Leprous with white scars where the grass has receded from the chalky soil. In contemplation of this erosion the eye finds solace. Everywhere stone is gaining. Whiteness. More and more every year. As well say every instant. Everywhere every instant whiteness is gaining.

The eye will return to the scene of its betrayals. On centennial leave from where tears freeze. Free again an instant to shed them scalding. On the blest tears once shed. While exulting at the white heap of stone. Ever heaping for want of better on itself. Which if it persist will gain the skies. The moon. Venus.

From the stones she steps down into the pastures. As from one tier of a circus to the next. A gap time will fill. For faster than the stones invade it the other ground upheaves its own. So far in silence. A silence time will break. This great silence evening and night. Then all along the verge the muffled thud of stone on stone. Of those spilling their excess on those emergent. Only now and then at first. Then at ever briefer intervals. Till one continuous din. With none to hear. Decreasing as the levels draw together to silence once again. Evening and night. In the meantime she is suddenly sitting with her feet in the pastures. Were it not for the empty hands on the way who knows to the tomb. Back from it then more likely. On the way back from the tomb. Frozen true to her wont she seems turned to stone. Face to the further confines the eye closes in vain to see. At last they appear an instant. North where she passes them always. Shroud of radiant haze. Where to melt into paradise.

The long white hair stares in a fan. Above and about the impassive face. Stares as if shocked still by some ancient horror. Or by its continuance. Or by another. That leaves the face stonecold. Silence at the eye of the scream. Which say? Ill say. Both. All three. Question answered.

Seated on the stones she is seen from behind. From the waist up. Trunk black rectangle. Nape under frill of black lace. White half halo of hair. Face to the north. The tomb. Eyes on the horizon perhaps. Or closed to see the headstone. The withered crocuses. Endless evening. She lit aslant by the last rays. They make no difference. None to the black of the cloth. None to the white hair. It too dead still. In the still air. Voidlike calm as always. Evening and night. Suffice to watch the grass. How motionless it droops. Till under the relentless eye it shivers. With faintest shiver from its innermost. Equally the hair. Rigidly horrent it shivers at last for the eye about to abandon. And the old body itself. When it seems of stone. Is it not in fact ashiver from head to foot? Let her but go and stand still by the other stone. It white from afar in the pastures. And the eye go from one to the other. Back and forth. What calm then. And what storm. Beneath the weeds' mock calm.

Not possible any longer except as figment. Not endurable. Nothing for it but to close the eye for good and see her. Her and the rest. Close it for good and all and see her to death. Unremittent. In the shack. Over the stones. In the pastures. The haze. At the tomb. And back. And the rest. For good and all. To death. Be shut of it all. On to the next. Next figment. Close it for good this filthy eye of flesh. What forbids? Careful.

Such—such fiasco that folly takes a hand. Such bits and scraps. Seen no matter how and said as seen. Dread of black. Of white. Of void. Let her vanish. And the rest. For good. And the sun. Last rays. And the moon. And Venus. Nothing left but black sky. White earth. Or inversely. No more sky or earth. Finished high and low. Nothing but black and white. Everywhere no matter where. But black. Void. Nothing else. Contemplate that. Not another word. Home at last. Gently gently.

Panic past pass on. The hands. Seen from above. They rest on the pubis intertwined. Strident white. Their faintly leaden tinge killed by the black ground. Suspicion of lace at the wrists. To go with the frill. They tighten then loosen their clasp. Slow systole diastole. And the body that scandal. While its sole hands in view. On its sole pubis. Dead still to be sure. On the chair. After the spectacle. Slowly its spell unbinding. On and on they keep. Tightening and loosening their clasp. Rhythm of a labouring heart. Till when almost despaired of gently part. Suddenly gently. Spreading rise and in midair palms uppermost come to rest. Behold our hollows. Then after a moment as if to hide the lines fall back pronating as they go and light flat on head of thighs. Within an ace of the crotch. It is now the left hand lacks its third finger. A swelling no doubt—a swelling no doubt of the knuckle between first and second phalanges preventing one panic day withdrawal of the ring. The kind called keeper. Still as stones they defy as stones do the eye. Do they as much as feel the clad flesh? Does the clad flesh feel them? Will they then never quiver? This night assuredly not. For before they have—before the eye has time they mist. Who is to blame? Or what? They? The eye? The missing finger? The keeper? The cry? What cry? All five. All six. And the rest. All. All to blame. All.

Winter evening in the pastures. The snow has ceased. Her steps so light they barely leave a trace. Have barely left having ceased. Just enough to be still visible. Adrift the snow. Whither in her head while her feet stray thus? Hither and thither too? Or unswerving to the mirage? And where when she halts? The eye discerns afar a kind of stain. Finally the steep roof whence part of the fresh fall has slid. Under the low lowering sky the north is lost. Obliterated by the snow the twelve are there. Invisible were she to raise her eyes. She on the contrary immaculately black. Not having received a single flake. Nothing needed now but for them to start falling again which therefore they do. First one by one here and there. Then thicker and thicker plumb through the still air. Slowly she disappears. Together with the trace of her steps and that of the distant roof. How find her way home? Home! Even as the homing bird. Safe as the saying is and sound.

All dark in the cabin while she whitens afar. Silence but for the imaginary murmur of flakes beating on the roof. And every now and then a real creak. Her company. Here without having to close the eye sees her afar. Motionless in the snow under the snow. The buttonhook trembles from its nail as if a night like any other. Facing the black curtain the chair exudes its solitude. For want of a fellow-table. Far from it in a corner see suddenly an antique coffer. In its therefore no lesser solitude. It perhaps that creaks. And in its depths who knows the key. The key to close. But this night the chair.

Its immovable air. Less than the—more than the empty seat the barred back is piteous. Here if she eats here she sits to eat. The eye closes in the dark and sees her in the end. With her right hand as large as life she holds the edge of the bowl resting on her knees. With her left the spoon dipped in the slop. She waits. For it to cool perhaps. But no. Merely frozen again just as about to begin. At last in a twin movement full of grace she slowly raises the bowl toward her lips while at the same time with equal slowness bowing her head to join it. Having set out at the same instant they meet halfway and there come to rest. Fresh rigor before the first spoonful slobbered largely back into the slop. Others no happier till time to part lips and bowl and slowly back with never a slip to their starting points. As smooth and even fro as to. Now again the rigid Memnon pose. With her right hand she holds the edge of the bowl. With her left the spoon dipped in the slop. So far so good. But before she can proceed she fades and disappears. Nothing now for the staring eye but the chair in its solitude.

One evening she was followed by a lamb. Reared for slaughter like the others it left them to follow her. In the present to conclude. All so bygone. Slaughter apart it is not like the others. Hanging to the ground in matted coils its fleece hides the little shanks. Rather than walk it seems to glide like a toy in tow. It halts at the same instant as she. At the same instant as she strays on. Stockstill as she it waits with head like hers extravagantly bowed. Clash of black and white that far from muting the last rays amplify. It is now her puniness leaps to the eye. Thanks it would seem to the lowly creature next her. Brief paradox. For suddenly together they move on. Hither and thither toward the stones. There she turns and sits. Does she see the white body at her feet? Head haught now she gazes into emptiness. That profusion. Or with closed eyes sees the tomb. The lamb goes no further. Alone night fallen she makes for home. Home! As straight as were it to be seen.

Was it ever over and done with questions? Dead the whole brood no sooner hatched. Long before. In the egg. Long before. Over and done with answering. With not being able. With not being able not to want to know. With not being able. No. Never. A dream. Question answered.

***

What remains for the eye exposed to such conditions? To such vicissitude of hardly there and wholly gone. Why none but to open no more. Till all done. She done. Or left undone. Tenement and unreason. No more unless to rest. In the outward and so-called visible. That daub. Quick again to the brim the old nausea and shut again. On her. Till she be whole. Or abort. Question answered.

The coffer. Empty after long nocturnal search. Nothing. Save in the end in a cranny of dust a scrap of paper. Jagged along one edge as if torn from a diary. On its yellowed face in barely legible ink two letters followed by a number. Tu 17. Or Th. Tu or Th 17. Otherwise blank. Otherwise empty.

She reemerges on her back. Dead still. Evening and night. Dead still on her back evening and night. The bed. Careful. A pallet? Hardly if head as ill seen when on her knees. Praying if she prays. Pah she has only to grovel deeper. Or grovel elsewhere. Before the chair. Or the coffer. Or at the edge of the pastures with her head on the stones. A pallet then flat on the floor. No pillow.

Hidden from chin to foot under a black covering she offers her face alone. Alone! Face defenceless evening and night. Quick the eyes. The moment they open. Suddenly they are there. Nothing having stirred. One is enough. One staring eye. Gaping pupil thinly nimbed with washen blue. No trace of humour. None any more. Unseeing. As if dazed by what seen behind the lids. The other plumbs its dark. Then opens in its turn. Dazed in its turn.

Incontinent the void. The zenith. Evening again. When not night it will be evening. Death again of deathless day. On the one hand embers. On the other ashes. Day without end won and lost. Unseen.

On resumption the head is covered. No matter. No matter now. Such the confusion now between real and—how say its contrary? No matter. That old tandem. Such now the confusion between them once so twain. And such the farrago from eye to mind. For it to make what sad sense of it may. No matter now. Such equal liars both. Real and—how ill say its contrary? The counter-poison.

***

Still fresh the coffer fiasco what now of all things but a trapdoor. So cunningly contrived that even to the lidded eye it scarcely shows. Careful. Raise it at once and risk another rebuff? No question. Simply savour in advance with in mind the grisly cupboard its conceivable contents. For the first time then wooden floor. Its boards in line with the trap's designed to conceal it. Promising this flagrant concern with camouflage. But beware. Question by the way what wood of all woods? Ebony why not? Ebony boards. Black on black the brushing skirt. Stark the skeleton chair death-paler than life.

While head included she lies hidden time for a turn in the pastures. No shock were she already dead. As of course she is. But in the meantime more convenient not. Still living then she lies hidden. Having for some reason covered her head. Or for no reason. Night. When not evening night. Winter night. No snow. For the sake of variety. To vary the monotony. The limp grass strangely rigid under the weight of the rime. Clawed by the long black skirt how if but heard it must murmur. Moonless star-studded sky reflected in the erosions filmed with ice. The silence merges into music infinitely far and as unbroken as silence. Ceaseless celestial winds in unison. For all all matters now. The stones gleam faintly afar and the cabin walls seen white at last. Said white. The guardians—the twelve are there but not at full muster. Well! Above all not understand. Simply note now those still faithful have moved apart. Such ill seen that night in the pastures. While head included she lies hidden. Under on closer inspection a long greatcoat. A man's by the buttons. The buttonholes. Eyes closed does she see him?

White walls. High time. White as new. No wind. Not a breath. Unbeaten on by all that comes beating down. And mystery the sun has spared them. The sun that once beat down. So east and west sides the required clash. South gable no problem. But the other. That door. Careful. Black too? Black too. And the roof. Slates. More. Small slates black too brought from a ruined mansion. What tales had they tongues to tell. Their long tale told. Such the dwelling ill seen ill said. Outwardly. High time.

***

Changed the stone that draws her when revisited alone. Or she who changes it when side by side. Now alone it leans. Backward or forward as the case may be. Is it to nature alone it owes its rough-hewn air? Or to some too human hand forced to desist? As Michelangelo's from the regicide's bust. If there may not be no more questions let there at least be no more answers. Granite of no common variety assuredly. Black as jade the jasper that flecks its whiteness. On its what is the wrong word its uptilted face obscure graffiti. Scrawled by the ages for the eye to solicit in vain. Winter evenings on her doorstep she imagines she can see it glitter afar. When from their source in the west-south-west the last rays rake its averse face. Such ill seen the stone alone where it stands at the far fringe of the pastures. On her way out with the flowers as unerring as best she can she lingers by it. As on her way back with empty hands. Lingers by it a while on her way on. Toward the one or other abode. As unerring as best she can.

See them again side by side. Not quite touching. Lit aslant by the latest last rays they cast to the east-north-east their long parallel shadows. Evening therefore.

Winter evening. It will always be evening. Always winter. When not night. Winter night. No more lambs. No more flowers. Empty-handed she shall go to the tomb. Until she go no more. Or no more return. So much for that. Undistinguishable the twin shadows. Till one at length more dense as if of a body better opaque. At length more still. As faintly at length the other trembles under the staring gaze. Throughout this confrontation the sun stands still. That is to say the earth. Not to recoil on until the parting. Then on its face over the pastures and then the stones the still living shadow slowly glides. Lengthening and fading more and more. But never quite away. Under the hovering eye.

Close-up of a dial. Nothing else. White disc divided in minutes. Unless it be in seconds. Sixty black dots. No figure. One hand only. Finest of fine black darts. It advances by fits and starts. No tick. Leaps from dot to dot with so lightning a leap that but for its new position it had not stirred. Whole nights may pass as may but a fraction of a second or any intermediate lapse of time soever before it flings itself from one degree to the next. None at any moment overleaping in all fairness be it said. Let it when discovered be pointing east. Having thus covered after its fashion assuming the instrument plumb the first quarter of its latest hour. Unless it be its latest minute. Then doubt certain—then despair certain nights of its ever attaining the last. Ever regaining north.

She reappears at evening at her window. When not night evening. If she will see Venus again she must open it. Well! First draw aside the curtain and then open. Head bowed she waits to be able. Mindful perhaps of evenings when she was able too late. Black night fallen. But no. In her head too pure wait. The curtain. Seen closer thanks to this hiatus it reveals itself at last for what it is. A black greatcoat. Hooked by its tails from the rod it hangs sprawling inside out like a carcass in a butcher's stall. Or better inside in for the pathos of the dangling arms. Same infinitesimal quaver as the buttonhook and passim. Another novelty the chair drawn up to the window. This to raise the line of sight on the fair prey loftier when first sighted than at first sight ill seen. What empty space henceforward. For long pacing to and fro in the gloom. Suddenly in a single gesture she snatches aside the coat and to again on a sky as black as it. And then?

Careful. Have her sit? Lie? Kneel? Go? She too vacillates. Till in the end the back and forth prevails. Sends her wavering north and south from wall to wall. In the kindly dark.

She is vanishing. With the rest. The already ill seen be-dimmed and ill seen again annulled. The mind betrays the treacherous eyes and the treacherous word their treacheries. Haze sole certitude. The same that reigns beyond the pastures. It gains them already. It will gain the zone of stones. Then the dwelling through all its chinks. The eye will close in vain. To see but haze. Not even. Be itself but haze. How can it ever be said? Quick how ever ill said before it submerges all. Light. In one treacherous word. Dazzling haze. Light in its might at last. Where no more to be seen. To be said. Gently gently.

The face yet again in the light of the last rays. No loss of pallor. None of cold. Suspended on the verge for this sight the westering sun. That is the eastering earth. The thin lips seem as if never again to part. Peeping from their join a suspicion of pulp. Unlikely site of olden kisses given and received. Or given only. Or received only. Impressive above all the corners imperceptibly upcurved. A smile? Is it possible? Ghost of an ancient smile smiled finally once and for all. Such ill half seen the mouth in the light of the last rays. Suddenly they leave it. Rather it leaves them. Off again to the dark. There to smile on. If smile is what it is.

Reexamined rid of light the mouth changes. Unexplainably. Lips as before. Same closure. Same hint of extruding pulp. At the corners same imperceptible laxness. In a word the smile still there if smile is what it is. Neither more nor less. Less! And yet no longer the same. True that light distorts. Particularly sunset. That mockery. True too that the eyes then agaze for the viewless planet are now closed. On other viewlessness. Of which more if ever anon. There the explanation at last. This same smile established with eyes open is with them closed no longer the same. Though between the two inspections the mouth unchanged. Utterly. Good. But in what way no longer the same? What there now that was not there? What there no more that was? Enough. Away.

* * *

Back after many winters. Long after in this endless winter. This endless heart of winter. Too soon. She as when fled. Where as when fled. Still or again. Eyes closed in the dark. To the dark. In their own dark. On the lips same minute smile. If smile is what it is. In short alive as she alone knows how neither more nor less. Less! Compared to true stone. Within as sadly as before all as at first sight ill seen. With the happy exception of the lights' enhanced opacity. Dim the light of day from them were day again to dawn. Without on the other hand some progress. Toward unbroken night. Universal stone. Day no sooner risen fallen. Scrapped all the ill seen ill said. The eye has changed. And its drivelling scribe. Absence has changed them. Not enough. Time to go again. Where still more to change. Whence back too soon. Changed but not enough. Strangers but not enough. To all the ill seen ill said. Then back again. Disarmed for to finish with it all at last. With her and her rags of sky and earth. And if again too soon go again. Change still more again. Then back again. Barring impediment. Ah. So on. Till fit to finish with it all at last. All the trash. In unbroken night. Universal stone. So first go. But first see her again. As when fled. And the abode. That under the changed eye it too may change. Begin. Just one parting look. Before all meet again. Then go. Barring impediment. Ah.

But see she suddenly no longer there. Where suddenly fled. Quick then the chair before she reappears. At length. Every angle. With what one word convey its change? Careful. Less. Ah the sweet one word. Less. It is less. The same but less. Whencesoever the glare. True that the light. See now how words too. A few drops mishaphazard. Then strangury. To say the least. Less. It will end by being no more. By never having been. Divine prospect. True that the light.

Suddenly enough and way for remembrance. Closed again to that end the vile jelly or opened again or left as it was however that was. Till all recalled. First finally by far hanging from their skirts two black greatcoats. Followed by the first hazy outlines of what possibly a hutch when suddenly enough. Remembrance! When all worse there than when first ill seen. The pallet. The chair. The coffer. The trap. Alone the eye has changed. Alone can cause to change. In the meantime nothing wanting.

Wrong. The buttonhook. The nail. Wrong. There they are again. Still. Worse there than ever. Unchanged for the worse. Ope eye and at them to begin. But first the partition. It rid they too would be. It less they by as much.

It of all the properties doubtless the least obdurate. See the instant see it again when unaided it dissolved. So to say of itself. With no help from the eye. Not till long after to reappear. As if reluctantly. For what reason? For one not far to seek. For others then said obscure. One other above all. One other still far to seek. Analogy of the heart? The skull? Hear from here the howls of laughter of the damned.

Enough. Quicker. Quick see how all in keeping with the chair. Minimally less. No more. Well on the way to inexistence. As to zero the infinite. Quick say. And of her? As much. Quick find her again. In that black heart. That mock brain.

***

The sheet. Between tips of trembling fingers. In two.
Four. Eight. Old frantic fingers. Not paper any more.
Each eighth apart. In two. Four. Finish with the knife.
Hack into shreds. Down the plughole. On to the next.
White. Quick blacken.

Alone the face remains. Of the rest beneath its covering
no trace. During the inspection a sudden sound. Startling without consequence for the gaze the mind awake.
How explain it? And without going so far how say it?
Far behind the eye the quest begins. What time the event
recedes. When suddenly to the rescue it comes again.
Forthwith the uncommon common noun collapsion.
Reinforced a little later if not enfeebled by the infrequent
slumberous. A slumberous collapsion. Two. Then far
from the still agonizing eye a gleam of hope. By the grace
of these modest beginnings. With in second sight the
shack in ruins. To scrute together with the inscrutable
face. All curiosity spent.

Later while the face still unyielding another sound of fall
but this time sharp. Heightening the fond illusion of

general havoc in train. Here a great leap into what brief future remains and summary puncture of that puny balloon. Far ahead to the instant when the coats will have gone from their rods and the buttonhook from its nail. And been hove the sigh no more than that. Sigh upon sigh till all sighed quite away. All the fond trash. Destined before being to be no more than that. Last sighs. Of relief.

Quick beforehand again two mysteries. Not even. Mild shocks. Not even. In such abeyance the mind then. And from then on. First the curtains gone without loss of dark. Sweet foretaste of the joy at journey's end. Second after long hesitation no trace of the fallen where they fell. No trace of all the ado. Alone on the one hand the rods alone. A little bent. And alone on the other most alone the nail. Unimpaired. All set to serve again. Like unto its glorious ancestors. At the place of the skull. One April afternoon. Deposition done.

Full glare now on the face present throughout the recent future. As seen ill seen throughout the past neither more nor less. Less! Collated with its cast it lives beyond a doubt. Were it only by virtue of its imperfect pallor. And imperceptible tremor unworthy of true plaster. Heartening on the other hand the eyes persistently closed. No doubt a record in this position. Unobserved at least till now. Suddenly the look. Nothing having stirred. Look? Too weak a word. Too wrong. Its absence? No better. Unspeakable globe. Unbearable.

Ample time none the less a few seconds for the iris to be lacking. Wholly. As if engulfed by the pupil. And for the sclerotic not to say the white to appear reduced by half. Already that much less at least but at what cost. Soon to be foreseen save unforeseen two black blanks. Fit ventholes of the soul that jakes. Here reappearance of the skylights opaque to no purpose henceforward. Seeing the black night or better blackness pure and simple that limpid they would shed. Blackness in its might at last. Where no more to be seen. Perforce to be seen.

Absence supreme good and yet. Illumination then go again and on return no more trace. On earth's face. Of what was never. And if by mishap some left then go again. For good again. So on. Till no more trace. On earth's face. Instead of always the same place. Slaving away forever in the same place. At this and that trace. And what if the eye could not? No more tear itself away from the remains of trace. Of what was never. Quick say it suddenly can and farewell say say farewell. If only to the face. Of her tenacious trace.

Decision no sooner reached or rather long after than what is the wrong word? For the last time at last for to end yet again what the wrong word? Than revoked. No but slowly dispelled a little very little like the last wisps of day when the curtain closes. Of itself by slow milli-metres or drawn by a phantom hand. Farewell to fare-well. Then in that perfect dark foreknell darling sound pip for end begun. First last moment. Grant only enough remain to devour all. Moment by glutton moment. Sky earth the whole kit and boodle. Not another crumb of carrion left. Lick chops and basta. No. One moment more. One last. Grace to breathe that void. Know happiness.

Worstward Ho

On. Say on. Be said on. Somehow on. Till nohow on. Said nohow on.

Say for be said. Missaid. From now say for be missaid.

Say a body. Where none. No mind. Where none. That at least. A place. Where none. For the body. To be in. Move in. Out of. Back into. No. No out. No back. Only in. Stay in. On in. Still.

All of old. Nothing else ever. Ever tried. Ever failed. No matter. Try again. Fail again. Fail better.

***

First the body. No. First the place. No. First both. Now
either. Now the other. Sick of the either try the other.
Sick of it back sick of the either. So on. Somehow on.
Till sick of both. Throw up and go. Where neither. Till
sick of there. Throw up and back. The body again. Where
none. The place again. Where none. Try again. Fail again.
Better again. Or better worse. Fail worse again. Still worse
again. Till sick for good. Throw up for good. Go for good.
Where neither for good. Good and all.

It stands. What? Yes. Say it stands. Had to up in the
end and stand. Say bones. No bones but say bones.
Say ground. No ground but say ground. So as to say
pain. No mind and pain? Say yes that the bones may pain
till no choice but stand. Somehow up and stand. Or
better worse remains. Say remains of mind where none
to permit of pain. Pain of bones till no choice but up
and stand. Somehow up. Somehow stand. Remains of
mind where none for the sake of pain. Here of bones.
Other examples if needs must. Of pain. Relief from.
Change of.

***

All of old. Nothing else ever. But never so failed. Worse failed. With care never worse failed.

Dim light source unknown. Know minimum. Know nothing no. Too much to hope. At most mere minimum. Mere-most minimum.

No choice but stand. Somehow up and stand. Somehow stand. That or groan. The groan so long on its way. No. No groan. Simply pain. Simply up. A time when try how. Try see. Try say. How first it lay. Then somehow knelt. Bit by bit. Then on from there. Bit by bit. Till up at last. Not now. Fail better worse now.

Another. Say another. Head sunk on crippled hands. Vertex vertical. Eyes clenched. Seat of all. Germ of all.

No future in this. Alas yes.

***

It stands. See in the dim void how at last it stands. In the dim light source unknown. Before the downcast eyes. Clenched eyes. Staring eyes. Clenched staring eyes.

That shade. Once lying. Now standing. That a body? Yes. Say that a body. Somehow standing. In the dim void.

A place. Where none. A time when try see. Try say. How small. How vast. How if not boundless bounded. Whence the dim. Not now. Know better now. Unknow better now. Know only no out of. No knowing how know only no out of. Into only. Hence another. Another place where none. Whither once whence no return. No. No place but the one. None but the one where none. Whence never once in. Somehow in. Beyondless. Thenceless there. Thitherless there. Thenceless thitherless there.

Where then but there see—

***

See for be seen. Misseen. From now see for be misseen.

Where then but there see now—

First back turned the shade astand. In the dim void see first back turned the shade astand. Still.

Where then but there see now another. Bit by bit an old man and child. In the dim void bit by bit an old man and child. Any other would do as ill.

Hand in hand with equal plod they go. In the free hands — no. Free empty hands. Backs turned both bowed with equal plod they go. The child hand raised to reach the holding hand. Hold the old holding hand. Hold and be held. Plod on and never recede. Slowly with never a pause plod on and never recede. Backs turned. Both bowed. Joined by held holding hands. Plod on as one. One shade. Another shade.

***

Head sunk on crippled hands. Clenched staring eyes. At
in the dim void shades. One astand at rest. One old man
and child. At rest plodding on. Any others would do as
ill. Almost any. Almost as ill.

They fade. Now the one. Now the twain. Now both.
Fade back. Now the one. Now the twain. Now both.
Fade? No. Sudden go. Sudden back. Now the one. Now
the twain. Now both.

Unchanged? Sudden back unchanged? Yes. Say yes. Each
time unchanged. Somehow unchanged. Till no. Till say
no. Sudden back changed. Somehow changed. Each
time somehow changed.

The dim. The void. Gone too? Back too? No. Say no.
Never gone. Never back. Till yes. Till say yes. Gone too.
Back too. The dim. The void. Now the one. Now the
other. Now both. Sudden gone. Sudden back. Unchanged? Sudden back unchanged? Yes. Say yes. Each

94

time unchanged. Somehow unchanged. Till no. Till say no. Sudden back changed. Somehow changed. Each time somehow changed.

First sudden gone the one. First sudden back. Unchanged. Say now unchanged. So far unchanged. Back turned. Head sunk. Vertex vertical in hat. Cocked back of black brim alone. Back of black greatcoat cut off midthigh. Kneeling. Better kneeling. Better worse kneeling. Say now kneeling. From now kneeling. Could rise but to its knees. Sudden gone sudden back unchanged back turned head sunk dark shade on unseen knees. Still.

Next sudden gone the twain. Next sudden back. Unchanged. Say now unchanged. So far unchanged. Backs turned. Heads sunk. Dim hair. Dim white and hair so fair that in that dim light dim white. Black greatcoats to heels. Dim black. Bootheels. Now the two right. Now the two left. As on with equal plod they go. No ground. Plod as on void. Dim hands. Dim white. Two free and two as one. So sudden gone sudden back unchanged as one dark shade plod unreceding on.

***

The dim. Far and wide the same. High and low. Unchanging. Say now unchanging. Whence no knowing. No saying. Say only such dim light as never. On all. Say a grot in that void. A gulf. Then in that grot or gulf such dimmest light as never. Whence no knowing. No saying.

The void. Unchanging. Say now unchanging. Void were not the one. The twain. So far were not the one and twain. So far.

The void. How try say? How try fail? No try no fail. Say only—

First the bones. On back to them. Preying since first said on foresaid remains. The ground. The pain. No bones. No ground. No pain. Why up unknown. At all costs unknown. If ever down. No choice but up if ever down. Or never down. Forever kneeling. Better forever kneeling. Better worse forever kneeling. Say from now forever kneeling. So far from now forever kneeling. So far.

* * *

The void. Before the staring eyes. Stare where they may. Far and wide. High and low. That narrow field. Know no more. See no more. Say no more. That alone. That little much of void alone.

On back to unsay void can go. Void cannot go. Save dim go. Then all go. All not already gone. Till dim back. Then all back. All not still gone. The one can go. The twain can go. Dim can go. Void cannot go. Save dim go. Then all go.

On back better worse to fail the head said seat of all. Germ of all. All? If of all of it too. Where if not there it too? There in the sunken head the sunken head. The hands. The eyes. Shade with the other shades. In the same dim. The same narrow void. Before the staring eyes. Where it too if not there too? Ask not. No. Ask in vain. Better worse so.

* * *

The head. Ask not if it can go. Say no. Unasking no. It cannot go. Save dim go. Then all go. Oh dim go. Go for good. All for good. Good and all.

Whose words? Ask in vain. Or not in vain if say no knowing. No saying. No words for him whose words. Him? One. No words for one whose words. One? It. No words for it whose words. Better worse so.

Something not wrong with one. Meaning—meaning! —meaning the kneeling one. From now one for the kneeling one. As from now two for the twain. The as one plodding twain. As from now three for the head. The head as first said missaid. So from now. For to gain time. Time to lose. Gain time to lose. As the soul once. The world once.

Something not wrong with one. Then with two. Then with three. So on. Something not wrong with all. Far from wrong. Far far from wrong.

***

The words too whosesoever. What room for worse! How almost true they sometimes almost ring! How wanting in inanity! Say the night is young alas and take heart. Or better worse say still a watch of night alas to come. A rest of last watch to come. And take heart.

First one. First try fail better one. Something there badly not wrong. Not that as it is it is not bad. The no face bad. The no hands bad. The no——. Enough. A pox on bad. Mere bad. Way for worse. Pending worse still. First worse. Mere worse. Pending worse still. Add a——. Add? Never. Bow it down. Be it bowed down. Deep down. Head in hat gone. More back gone. Greatcoat cut off higher. Nothing from pelvis down. Nothing but bowed back. Topless baseless hindtrunk. Dim black. On unseen knees. In the dim void. Better worse so. Pending worse still.

Next try fail better two. The twain. Bad as it is as it is. Bad the no——

First back on to three. Not yet to try worsen. Simply be there again. There in that head in that head. Be it again.

That head in that head. Clenched eyes clamped to it alone. Alone? No. Too. To it too. The sunken skull. The crippled hands. Clenched staring eyes. Clenched eyes clamped to clenched staring eyes. Be that shade again. In that shade again. With the other shades. Worsening shades. In the dim void.

Next—

First how all at once. In that stare. The worsened one. The worsening two. And what yet to worsen. To try worsen. Itself. The dim. The void. All at once in that stare. Clenched eyes clamped to all.

Next two. From bad to worsen. Try worsen. From merely bad. Add—. Add? Never. The boots. Better worse bootless. Bare heels. Now the two right. Now the two left. Left right left right on. Barefoot unreceding on. Better worse so. A little better worse than nothing so.

Next the so-said seat and germ of all. Those hands! That head! That near true ring! Away. Full face from now.

No hands. No face. Skull and stare alone. Scene and seer of all.

On. Stare on. Say on. Be on. Somehow on. Anyhow on. Till dim gone. At long last gone. All at long last gone. For bad and all. For poor best worse and all.

Dim whence unknown. At all costs unknown. Unchanging. Say now unchanging. Far and wide. High and low. Say a pipe in that void. A tube. Sealed. Then in that pipe or tube that selfsame dim. Old dim. When ever what else? Where all always to be seen. Of the nothing to be seen. Dimly seen. Nothing ever unseen. Of the nothing to be seen. Dimly seen. Worsen that?

Next the so-said void. The so-missaid. That narrow field. Rife with shades. Well so-missaid. Shade-ridden void. How better worse so-missay?

Add others. Add? Never. Till if needs must. Nothing to those so far. Dimly so far. Them only lessen. But with them as they lessen others. As they worsen. If needs must. Others to lessen. To worsen. Till dim go. At long last go. For worst and all.

On. Somehow on. Anyhow on. Say all gone. So on. In the skull all gone. All? No. All cannot go. Till dim go. Say then but the two gone. In the skull one and two gone. From the void. From the stare. In the skull all save the skull gone. The stare. Alone in the dim void. Alone to be seen. Dimly seen. In the skull the skull alone to be seen. The staring eyes. Dimly seen. By the staring eyes. The others gone. Long sudden gone. Then sudden back. Unchanged. Say now unchanged. First one. Then two. Or first two. Then one. Or together. Then all again together. The bowed back. The plodding twain. The skull. The stare. All back in the skull together. Unchanged. Stare clamped to all. In the dim void.

The eyes. Time to—

First on back to unsay dim can go. Somehow on back. Dim cannot go. Dim to go must go for good. True then

dim can go. If but for good. One can go not for good.
Two too. Three no if not for good. With dim gone for
good. Void no if not for good. With all gone for good.
Dim can worsen. Somehow worsen. Go no. If not for
good.

The eyes. Time to try worsen. Somehow try worsen.
Unclench. Say staring open. All white and pupil. Dim
white. White? No. All pupil. Dim black holes. Unwaver-
ing gaping. Be they so said. With worsening words. From
now so. Better than nothing so bettered for the worse.

Still dim still on. So long as still dim still somehow on.
Anyhow on. With worsening words. Worsening stare.
For the nothing to be seen. At the nothing to be seen.
Dimly seen. As now by way of somehow on where in
the nowhere all together? All three together. Where
there all three at last worse seen? Bowed back alone.
Barefoot plodding twain. Skull and lidless stare. Where
in the narrow vast? Say only vasts apart. In that narrow
void vasts of void apart. Worse better later.

***

What when words gone? None for what then. But say by way of somehow on somehow with sight to do. With less of sight. Still dim and yet—. No. Nohow so on. Say better worse words gone when nohow on. Still dim and nohow on. All seen and nohow on. What words for what then? None for what then. No words for what when words gone. For what when nohow on. Somehow nohow on.

Worsening words whose unknown. Whence unknown. At all costs unknown. Now for to say as worst they may only they only they. Dim void shades all they. Nothing save what they say. Somehow say. Nothing save they. What they say. Whosesoever whencesoever say. As worst they may fail ever worse to say.

Remains of mind then still. Enough still. Somewhose somewhere somehow enough still. No mind and words? Even such words. So enough still. Just enough still to joy. Joy! Just enough still to joy that only they. Only!

Enough still not to know. Not to know what they say. Not to know what it is the words it says say. Says? Secretes. Say better worse secretes. What it is the words

it secretes say. What the so-said void. The so-said dim.
The so-said shades. The so-said seat and germ of all.
Enough to know no knowing. No knowing what it is
the words it secretes say. No saying. No saying what it
all is they somehow say.

That said on back to try worse say the plodding twain.
Preying since last worse said on foresaid remains. But
what not on them preying? What seen? What said? What
of all seen and said not on them preying? True. True!
And yet say worst perhaps worst of all the old man and
child. That shade as last worse seen. Left right left right
barefoot unreceding on. They then the words. Back to
them now for want of better on and better fail. Worser
fail that perhaps of all the least. Least worse failed of all
the worse failed shades. Less worse than the bowed back
alone. The skull and lidless stare. Though they too for
worse. But what not for worse. True. True! And yet say
first the worst perhaps worst of all the old man and child.
Worst in need of worse. Worse in—

Blanks for nohow on. How long? Blanks how long till
somehow on? Again somehow on. All gone when
nohow on. Time gone when nohow on.

***

Worse less. By no stretch more. Worse for want of better less. Less best. No. Naught best. Best worse. No. Not best worse. Naught not best worse. Less best worse. No. Least. Least best worse. Least never to be naught. Never to naught be brought. Never by naught be nulled. Unnullable least. Say that best worse. With leastening words say least best worse. For want of worser worst. Unlessenable least best worse.

The twain. The hands. Held holding hands. That almost ring! As when first said on crippled hands the head. Crippled hands! They there then the words. Here now held holding. As when first said. Ununsaid when worse said. Away. Held holding hands!

The empty too. Away. No hands in the—. No. Save for worse to say. Somehow worse somehow to say. Say for now still seen. Dimly seen. Dim white. Two dim white empty hands. In the dim void.

***

So leastward on. So long as dim still. Dim undimmed. Or dimmed to dimmer still. To dimmost dim. Leastmost in dimmost dim. Utmost dim. Leastmost in utmost dim. Unworsenable worst.

What words for what then? How almost they still ring. As somehow from some soft of mind they ooze. From it in it ooze. How all but uninane. To last unlessenable least how loath to leasten. For then in utmost dim to unutter leastmost all.

So little worse the old man and child. Gone held holding hands they plod apart. Left right barefoot unreceding on. Not worsen yet the rift. Save for some after nohow somehow worser on.

On back to unsay clamped to all the stare. No but from now to now this and now that. As now from worsened twain to next for worse alone. To skull and stare alone. Of the two worse in want the skull preying since unsunk. Now say the fore alone. No dome. Temple to temple alone. Clamped to it and stare alone the stare. Bowed back alone and twain blurs in the void. So better than nothing worse shade three from now.

Somehow again on back to the bowed back alone. Nothing to show a woman's and yet a woman's. Oozed from softening soft the word woman's. The words old woman's. The words nothing to show bowed back alone a woman's and yet a woman's. So better worse from now that shade a woman's. An old woman's.

Next fail see say how dim undimmed to worsen. How nohow save to dimmer still. But but a shade so as when after nohow somehow on to dimmer still. Till dimmost dim. Best bad worse of all. Save somehow undimmed worser still.

Ooze on back not to unsay but say again the vasts apart. Say seen again. No worse again. The vasts of void apart. Of all so far missaid the worse missaid. So far. Not till nohow worse missay say worse missaid. Not till for good nohow on poor worst missaid.

***

Longing the so-said mind long lost to longing. The so-missaid. So far so-missaid. Dint of long longing lost to longing. Long vain longing. And longing still. Faintly longing still. Faintly vainly longing still. For fainter still. For faintest. Faintly vainly longing for the least of longing. Unlessenable least of longing. Unstillable vain last of longing still.

Longing that all go. Dim go. Void go. Longing go. Vain longing that vain longing go.

Said is missaid. Whenever said said said missaid. From now said alone. No more from now now said and now missaid. From now said alone. Said for missaid. For be missaid.

Back is on. Somehow on. From now back alone. No more from now now back and now back on. From now back alone. Back for back on. Back for somehow on.

***

Back unsay better worse by no stretch more. If more dim less light then better worse more dim. Unsaid then better worse by no stretch more. Better worse may no less than less be more. Better worse what? The say? The said. Same thing. Same nothing. Same all but nothing.

No once. No once in pastless now. No not none. When before worse the shades? The dim before more? When if not once. Onceless alone the void. By no stretch more. By none less. Onceless till no more.

Ooze back try worsen blanks. Those then when nohow on. Unsay then all gone. All not gone. Only nohow on. All not gone and nohow on. All there as now when somehow on. The dim. The void. The shades. Only words gone. Ooze gone. Till ooze again and on. Somehow ooze on.

Preying since last worse the stare. Something there still far so far from wrong. So far far far from wrong. Try better worse another stare when with words than when not. When somehow than when nohow. While all seen the same. No not all seen the same. Seen other. By the same other stare seen other. When with words than when not. When somehow than when nohow. How fail say how other seen?

Less. Less seen. Less seeing. Less seen and seeing when with words than when not. When somehow than when nohow. Stare by words dimmed. Shades dimmed. Void dimmed. Dim dimmed. All there as when no words. As when nohow. Only all dimmed. Till blank again. No words again. Nohow again. Then all undimmed. Stare undimmed. That words had dimmed.

Back unsay shades can go. Go and come again. No. Shades cannot go. Much less come again. Nor bowed old woman's back. Nor old man and child. Nor foreskull and stare. Blur yes. Shades can blur. When stare clamped to one alone. Or somehow words again. Go no nor come again. Till dim if ever go. Never to come again.

***

Blanks for when words gone. When nohow on. Then all seen as only then. Undimmed. All undimmed that words dim. All so seen unsaid. No ooze then. No trace on soft when from it ooze again. In it ooze again. Ooze alone for seen as seen with ooze. Dimmed. No ooze for seen undimmed. For when nohow on. No ooze for when ooze gone.

Back try worsen twain preying since last worse. Since atwain. Two once so one. From now rift a vast. Vast of void atween. With equal plod still unreceding on. That little better worse. Till words for worser still. Worse words for worser still.

Preying but what not preying? When not preying? Nohow over words again say what then when not preying. Each better worse for naught. No stilling preying. The shades. The dim. The void. All always faintly preying. Worse for naught. Worser for naught. No less than when but bad all always faintly preying. Gnawing.

***

Gnawing to be gone. Less no good. Worse no good. Only one good. Gone. Gone for good. Till then gnaw on. All gnaw on. To be gone.

All save void. No. Void too. Unworsenable void. Never less. Never more. Never since first said never unsaid never worse said never not gnawing to be gone.

Say child gone. As good as gone. From the void. From the stare. Void then not that much more? Say old man gone. Old woman gone. As good as gone. Void then not that much more again? No. Void most when almost. Worst when almost. Less then? All shades as good as gone. If then not that much more then that much less then? Less worse then? Enough. A pox on void. Unmoreable unlessable unworseable evermost almost void.

Back to once so-said two as one. Preying ever since not long since last failed worse. Ever since vast atween. Say better worse now all gone save trunks from now. Noth-

ing from pelves down. From napes up. Topless baseless hindtrunks. Legless plodding on. Left right
unreceding on.

Stare clamped to stare. Bowed backs blurs in stare
clamped to stare. Two black holes. Dim black. In
through skull to soft. Out from soft through skull. Agape
in unseen face. That the flaw? The want of flaw? Try
better worse set in skull. Two black holes in foreskull.
Or one. Try better still worse one. One dim black hole
mid-foreskull. Into the hell of all. Out from the hell of
all. So better than nothing worse say stare from now.

Stare outstared away to old man hindtrunk unreceding
on. Try better worse kneeling. Legs gone say better worse
kneeling. No more if ever on. Say never. Say never on.
Ever kneeling. Legs gone from stare say better worse ever
kneeling. Stare away to child and worsen same. Vast void
apart old man and child dim shades on unseen knees. One
blur. One clear. Dim clear. Now the one. Now the other.

***

Nothing to show a child and yet a child. A man and yet a man. Old and yet old. Nothing but ooze how nothing and yet. One bowed back yet an old man's. The other yet a child's. A small child's.

Somehow again and all in stare again. All at once as once. Better worse all. The three bowed down. The stare. The whole narrow void. No blurs. All clear. Dim clear. Black hole agape on all. Inletting all. Outletting all.

Nothing and yet a woman. Old and yet old. On unseen knees. Stooped as loving memory some old gravestones stoop. In that old graveyard. Names gone and when to when. Stoop mute over the graves of none.

Same stoop for all. Same vasts apart. Such last state. Latest state. Till somehow less in vain. Worse in vain. All gnawing to be naught. Never to be naught.

What were skull to go? As good as go. Into what then black hole? From out what then? What why of all? Bet-

ter worse so? No. Skull better worse. What left of skull.
Of soft. Worst why of all of all. So skull not go. What
left of skull not go. Into it still the hole. Into what left
of soft. From out what little left.

Enough. Sudden enough. Sudden all far. No move and
sudden all far. All least. Three pins. One pinhole. In
dimmost dim. Vasts apart. At bounds of boundless void.
Whence no farther. Best worse no farther. Nohow less.
Nohow worse. Nohow naught. Nohow on.

Said nohow on.